喚醒你的英文語感！

Get a Feel for English !

# 英文字彙多角建構

作者／白安竹
Andrew E. Bennett

# C O N T E N T S

4

# 本書使用方法

## 一、準備多益測驗與提升英語單字力同時進行

　　本書大部分的單字主題，與多益測驗的頻考主題相符。包括日常話題、辦公室、商務、人事、金融、交通、旅遊、導覽、運動休閒等。是準備多益考試者可以充分利用的單字學習書，但是必須強調的是，本書的單字學習絕對不只能幫助考試，而是能讓讀者真正學會使用英文。

## 二、規劃 1 個月（30 天）的學習份量，方便讀者控管學習進度。

　　每一課的內容都包含了：兩篇有趣的情境對話、10 個核心字彙與例句、10 個進階字彙、5 題填空練習題。須要花費的時間因人而異，大約在 30 分鐘到 1 個小時左右。如果想要反覆的聽 MP3 作聽力與口說練習，可能會需要更多時間，但是這樣的練習對讀者開口說英文有相當大的幫助，同時也能準備多益考試的聽力測驗。

　　本書的核心單字共有 300 個，進階單字也有 300 個。數量不多，但是能夠發揮這些核心單字的力量，必然比死記生字列表更有成效。

## 三、善用每個小單元，多層次學習字彙，達到最高學習成效

**Step 1** → 從情境對話開始接觸單字

和文章或例句比起來，「對話」是我們接觸外語最簡單的方式。因為有前後文和情境能幫助我們了解意思，而且又不像文章的句子那麼長。每一課有兩篇精選的情境對話，篇幅都不長，而且有故事性，

所以一次讀完也不會有壓力。

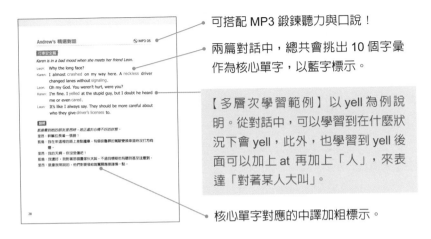

可搭配 MP3 鍛鍊聽力與口說！

兩篇對話中，總共會挑出 10 個字彙作為核心單字，以藍字標示。

【多層次學習範例】以 yell 為例說明。從對話中，可以學習到在什麼狀況下會 yell，此外，也學習到 yell 後面可以加上 at 再加上「人」，來表達「對著某人大叫」。

核心單字對應的中譯加粗標示。

**Step 2** → 將對話中的 10 個核心單字做延伸學習

核心單字皆列出音標、詞性、中譯、例句等資訊。特別之處在於，此處所列出的例句，完全不同於前面情境對話的句子。

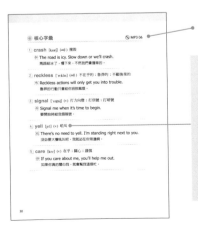

可搭配 MP3 聽例句！

【多層次學習範例】一樣以 yell 為例。在核心字彙呈現的例句讓讀者很容易就學到，這個字不只用在敘述 A 對著 B 大叫 (A yell at B) 這種行為，還可以用在勸人 "no need to yell"，所以，yell 這個字我們學到了第二個面向。

→ 補充進階字彙，學習再加廣

每一課的進階字彙有 10 個，通常是
與本課主題相關的延伸、擴充字。

【多層次學習範例】在進階單字的第二
個部份〔喊叫的方式〕列出了 yell 之外
的 5 種「喊叫」的相關動詞，scream、
shout、holler、bellow、roar，讀者可
以思考 scream（尖叫）等字跟 yell（大
叫）所表現出來的行為有何不同。

**Step 4** → Exercises 動手做，透過
對題目思考的過程來加深學習的印
象。

每一課的尾聲都是五題單字填充練
習，在這裡可以再次複習單字，並且
從不同的例句複習單字。

【多層次學習範例】第三題從後半句的
線索，讀者應該不難判斷選擇 yelling
作答。即使在做題目的同時，我們再度
學到 yell 這個字的不同面向，yell 可以
用來形容一個人的行徑。

**Step 5** → 每一章的單字總複習，提醒學習者做「循環式」的學習與複習。

讀者在一整章的學習之後，可能會有一些單字隨著時間而印象漸淺，此時即可利用本單元重新溫習。總複習的題目難度會比「Exercises 動手作」稍微升級一些，還會出現段落文字的填空。

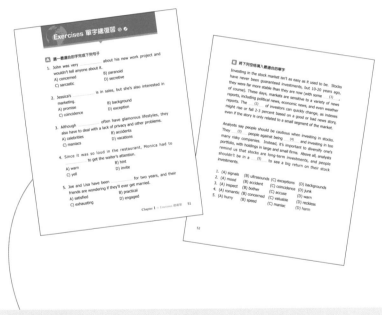

【多層次學習範例】第 4 題，由於讀者已經對 yell 有深入的學習，所以能輕易選出答案是 yell。並且又學到，在吵雜的環境中大聲叫人，也適用 yell 這個字。

本書作者是來自哈佛大學的教育專家，同時也是語言學習經驗非常豐富的實踐者！除了母語英文之外，他精通中文、日文、西班牙文、法文、德文。因此，由作者親力撰寫的獨門學習專欄是最有說服力的！讀者可以從中找到適合自己的學習方法與秘訣，您的語言學習將事半功倍。

好用的工具：單字檢索

在本書最後的「索引」，可以看到全書 600 個單字，從 A~Z 的順序排列，後面並加註該單字出現在哪一課，是系統化查找單字的好工具！

# Chapter 1
# 日常話題

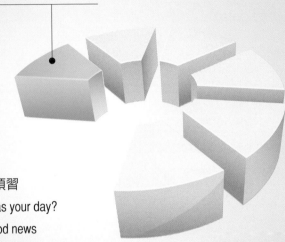

英語學習專欄 ❶
學習字彙的正確方法

## Preview 字彙預習

| | |
|---|---|
| beauty salon | 美容沙龍 |
| bother | 煩惱；打擾 |
| celebrity | 名人；名流 |
| coincidence | 巧合 |
| convenience store | 便利商店 |
| crazy | 荒謬的；瘋狂的 |
| demanding | 吃力的 |
| exhausting | 耗盡精力的 |
| extraordinary | 異常的 |
| fantastic | 極好的；極棒的 |
| hint | 提示 |
| inspect | 視察；檢查 |
| mood | 心情；情緒 |
| park | 公園 |
| pleasant | 愉快的 |
| pump | 用幫浦抽水 |
| restaurant | 餐廳 |
| roommate | 室友 |
| supermarket | 超市 |
| typical | 典型的 |

**夫妻生活篇**

*George works at a construction company. His wife greets him as he returns home.*

Sarah: How was your day?

George: Exhausting. I had to go by three different sites to inspect the work.

Sarah: That's crazy. When are they going to hire more people?

George: I keep asking them, but I never get an answer. I can't do the job by myself.

Sarah: I know. Listen, don't let that bother you now. Take your shoes off and relax on the sofa. I'll get you a beer.

**翻譯**

*喬治在一家建設公司做事，回到家時，他的老婆去迎接他。*

莎拉：你今天過得怎樣？

喬治：**忙得累死了**，我得到三個地方去**視察**工作進行的狀況。

莎拉：那太**荒謬**了，他們什麼時候才會多**僱**一點人？

喬治：我一直問他們，不過始終沒回應，我無法一個人做這個工作。

莎拉：我了解，你聽我說，現在別再**煩**那件事了，脫掉你的鞋子，在沙發上放鬆一下，我幫你拿罐啤酒。

老友篇

*Trisha walks through the door of her house with a big smile on her face.*

Mark: Somebody's in a good mood.

Trisha: Guess who I talked to at the gas station.

Mark: Who? A celebrity? The president? My mother? Come on, give me a hint.

Trisha: Mark, I don't think the president pumps his own gas. I saw my old college roommate, Ronda Wiley.

Mark: Now, that's a name I haven't heard for a long time. What a coincidence, your seeing her after all these years.

翻譯

*翠莎臉上充滿微笑地通過家門口。*

馬克：有人**心情**很好喔。

翠莎：你猜我在加油站跟誰說話了。

馬克：誰？某個**名人**？總統？我媽？拜託，給我一個**提示**吧。

翠莎：馬克，我想總統不會自己**加油**吧，我看到我**大學室友**，蓉達‧威利。

馬克：喔，我很久沒聽到那個名字了。經過這麼多年後你又遇見她，真的**好巧啊**。

① **exhausting** [ɪgˋzɔstɪŋ] (*adj.*) 耗盡精力的

例 I didn't realize how exhausting being a babysitter could be.
我以前並不了解當保母是這麼讓人精疲力竭。

② **inspect** [ɪnˋspɛkt] (*v.*) 視察；檢查

例 The health department plans to inspect our restaurant next week.
衛生局準備下週來檢查我們餐廳。

③ **crazy** [ˋkrezɪ] (*adj.*) 荒謬的；瘋狂的

例 They're crazy if they think the workers will accept a pay cut.
如果他們覺得員工們會接受減薪，他們就是瘋了。

④ **bother** [ˋbɑðɚ] (*v.*) 煩惱；打擾

例 Don't bother your sister. She's studying.
別打擾你姊姊，她在唸書。

⑤ **mood** [mud] (*n.*) 心情；情緒

例 Eating ice cream always puts Irvin in a good mood.
吃冰淇淋總是可以讓爾文心情很好。

⑥ **celebrity** [sə`lɛbrətɪ] (*n.*) 名人；名流

例 This magazine has all the latest gossip about the hottest celebrities.

這雜誌裡有所有當紅名人最新的八卦消息。

⑦ **hint** [hɪnt] (*n.*) 提示

例 If I give you a hint about where we're going, it'll ruin the surprise.

我如果提示你我們要去哪裡，那就會破壞這個驚喜了。

⑧ **pump** [pʌmp] (*v.*) 用幫浦抽水

例 This machine will pump all the water out of the hole we dug.

這機器會把我們挖的洞裡的水全部抽出來。

⑨ **roommate** [`rummet] (*n.*) 室友

例 Living with a roommate takes patience and understanding.

跟室友一起生活需要耐心與體諒。

⑩ **coincidence** [ko`ɪnsədəns] (*n.*) 巧合

例 I don't believe it was a coincidence. I think it was fate.

我不相信那是巧合，我倒覺得那是命運。

## 📌 進階字彙

形容一天過得如何的字

| | | | |
|---|---|---|---|
| **fantastic** | [fæn`tæstɪk] | *(adj.)* | 極好的；極棒的 |
| **typical** | [`tɪpɪkḷ] | *(adj.)* | 典型的 |
| **extraordinary** | [ɪk`strɔrdṇ ˌɛrɪ] | *(adj.)* | 異常的 |
| **pleasant** | [`plɛzəṇt] | *(adj.)* | 愉快的 |
| **demanding** | [dɪ`mændɪŋ] | *(adj.)* | 吃力的 |

常碰面的地方

| | | | |
|---|---|---|---|
| **supermarket** | [`supɚ `mɑrkɪt] | *(n.)* | 超市 |
| **park** | [pɑrk] | *(n.)* | 公園 |
| **beauty salon** | [`bjutɪ sa`lɔn] | *(n.)* | 美容沙龍 |
| **convenience store** | [kən`vinjəns `stor] | *(n.)* | 便利商店 |
| **restaurant** | [`rɛstərənt] | *(n.)* | 餐廳 |

文化總匯

在美國，很多人下課或下班後回到家裡，會跟家裡的人談起今天在學校或在公司的狀況，內容不外乎是遇到了什麼樣的問題、碰到什麼人、發生了什麼新鮮事，將自己的遭遇跟家人傾訴，藉以抒發自己的情緒。

# ✎ Exercises 動手做

請從以下字彙中，挑出正確的單字填入空格內。

| coincidence | exhausting | roommate | |
|---|---|---|---|
| inspect | bother | mood | hint |

1. We need to call someone to _____ the ceiling for cracks.

2. I know you're in a bad _____, but you don't have to yell at me.

3. Moving all these heavy boxes is _____.

4. Do you want a _____ about the present I bought you?

5. I doubt Brent followed you to the store. Your seeing him there was simply a _____.

1. 我們得叫人來檢查一下天花板的裂縫。
2. 我知道你心情不好，不過你也不必對我吼叫吧。
3. 搬這些重箱子真的很累人。
4. 你想要關於我買了什麼禮物給你的提示嗎？
5. 布蘭特真的有跟蹤你去店裡嗎？你會在那裡看到他只不過是巧合罷了。

解答 1. inspect  2. mood  3. exhausting  4. hint  5. coincidence

## Preview 字彙預習

| | |
|---|---|
| baby shower | 嬰兒慶生會 |
| bachelor's party | 單身漢之夜 |
| background | 背景；襯底 |
| best man | 伴郎 |
| brace | 支撐住；穩住 |
| bridal shower | 婚禮的聚會 |
| bride | 新娘 |
| bridesmaid | 伴娘 |
| candlelight | 燭光 |
| ceremony | 儀式；典禮 |
| engaged | 已經訂婚的 |
| exception | 例外；異議 |
| groom | 新郎 |
| honeymoon | 蜜月 |
| invite | 邀請 |
| priest | 神父；神職人員 |
| promise | 答應；承諾；保證 |
| reception | 歡迎會；招待會 |
| romantic | 浪漫的；多情的 |
| ultrasound | 超音波 |

〰〰〰〰〰〰〰〰〰〰〰〰〰〰〰〰〰〰〰〰〰〰〰〰〰〰〰〰〰〰

**訂婚篇**

*Kim has something important to tell her best friend.*

Judith: You sounded so excited on the phone. So, I'm waiting ...

Kim: Brace yourself, Gavin and I are engaged!

Judith: You got ... You're ... Oh my God! Wait, when did this happen?

Kim: Last night. We went to a romantic restaurant, with candlelight and soft music in the background. It was like something from a movie.

Judith: And you waited until today to tell me? Girl, next time you get engaged, I want you on the phone, calling me the moment it happens. No exceptions.

**翻譯**

*琴有重要的事要告訴她最好的朋友。*

朱蒂斯：妳電話裡的聲音聽起來好興奮，所以，我正等著妳說呢⋯⋯

琴　　：妳**準備**好喔，蓋文跟我**訂婚**了！

朱蒂斯：你們⋯⋯妳⋯⋯噢！我的天啊！等等，這是什麼時候發生的？

琴　　：昨晚。我們去了一家很**浪漫的**餐廳，有**燭**光和柔美的音樂做**陪襯**，就像電影裡的情節一樣。

朱蒂斯：而妳竟然等到今天才告訴我？女孩，下次妳訂婚的時候，我要妳在發生的那一刻就打電話跟我說，不許有**例外**。

生小孩篇

*Christopher has something special to tell one of his colleagues.*

Christopher: Guess what, Jill. I'm going to be a father.

Jill: Well, good for you. Do you know if it's a boy or a girl?

Christopher: Not yet. The ultrasound test is next week.

Jill: Make sure to invite me to the baby shower.

Christopher: I will. I promise.

翻譯

*克里斯多弗有個特別的消息要告訴他的同事。*

克里斯多弗：吉兒，妳猜怎麼著，我要當爸爸了。

吉兒　　　：喔，太好了，你知道孩子是男生還是女生嗎？

克里斯多弗：還不知道，下禮拜才要做**超音波**。

吉兒　　　：你一定要**邀**我去參加**嬰兒慶生**會喔。

克里斯多弗：我會的，我**保證**。

① **brace** [bres] (*v.*) 支撐住;做好準備;穩住

例 Everybody brace yourself! There's another big wave coming this way.

大家穩住啦!另一個大浪往這邊來啦。

---

② **engaged** [ɪn`gedʒd] (*adj.*) 已經訂婚的

例 I'm engaged to the greatest woman in the world.

我跟世界上最棒的女人訂婚了。

---

③ **romantic** [ro`mæntɪk] (*adj.*) 浪漫的;多情的

例 No, Sammy, Burger King is not my idea of a romantic restaurant.

不行,山米,我可不覺得漢堡王是浪漫的餐廳。

---

④ **candlelight** [`kændl͵laɪt] (*n.*) 燭光

例 Isn't reading by candlelight bad for your eyes?

用燭光看書不是對眼睛不好嗎?

---

⑤ **background** [`bæk͵graʊnd] (*n.*) 背景;襯底

例 I like the way this painting has trees and mountains in the background.

我喜歡這幅畫有樹有山當背景的樣子。

---

⑥ **exception** [ɪk`sɛpʃən] (*n.*) 例外；異議

例 No exceptions to the rule will be allowed.
這個規矩不許有任何例外。

⑦ **ultrasound** [`ʌltrə ˌsaʊnd] (*n.*) 超音波

例 Ultrasound tests have become a common part of most pregnancies.
照超音波已成為大多數懷孕過程中常見的一部分了。

⑧ **invite** [ɪn`vaɪt] (*v.*) 邀請

例 I want to invite 200 people to the wedding.
我想邀請兩百個人來參加婚禮。

⑨ **baby shower** [`bebɪ `ʃaʊɚ] (*n.*) 嬰兒慶生會

例 We're going to have so much fun at the baby shower.
我們在嬰兒慶生會時一定會有很多樂趣。

⑩ **promise** [`prɑmɪs] (*v.*) 答應；承諾；保證

例 Promise you'll call me as soon as you get home.
答應我你一到家就打電話給我。

### 🖈 進階字彙

#### 結婚相關事件

| | | |
|---|---|---|
| **bridal shower** | [`braɪd] `ʃauə] (*n.*) 婚禮的聚會 |
| **bachelor's party** | [`bætʃələz `pɑrtɪ] (*n.*) 單身漢之夜 |
| **ceremony** | [`sɛrə ˌmonɪ] (*n.*) 儀式；典禮 |
| **reception** | [rɪ`sɛpʃəl] (*n.*) 歡迎會；招待會 |
| **honeymoon** | [`hʌnɪ ˌmun] (*n.*) 蜜月 |

#### 婚禮相關人員

| | | |
|---|---|---|
| **bride** | [braɪd] (*n.*) 新娘 |
| **groom** | [grum] (*n.*) 新郎 |
| **best man** | [`bɛst `mæn] (*n.*) 伴郎 |
| **bridesmaid** | [`braɪdz ˌmæd] (*n.*) 伴娘 |
| **priest** | [prist] (*n.*) 神父；神職人員 |

在美國，嬰兒出生後人們通常會辦慶生會，性質很像台灣為出生滿月的嬰兒而請的滿月酒，不過參加嬰兒慶生會的人通常只有女性，她們會帶要送給嬰兒的禮物，像是一些奶粉、奶瓶、尿片、嬰兒衣服、嬰兒玩具等，這種聚會就叫 baby shower。

# ✐ Exercises 動手做

請從以下字彙中，挑出正確的單字填入空格內。

| engaged | candlelight | honeymoon | |
|---------|-------------|-----------|---|
| invite | brace | promise | romantic |

1. Going on a cruise sounds like such a _____ vacation.

2. This road is in very poor condition, so be sure to _____ yourself as we go down.

3. I can't believe you forgot to _____ your boss to your wedding!

4. We're _____, but we haven't decided exactly when we'll get married.

5. I _____ I'll tell you all about my honeymoon when I get back.

1. 郵輪假期聽起來很浪漫。

2. 這條路的路況很糟,路上你要坐穩。

3. 我不能相信你竟忘了要邀請你的老闆參加你的婚禮。

4. 我們已經訂婚了,不過還沒決定什麼時候結婚。

5. 我答應回來時會告訴你蜜月的全部事項。

解答 1. romantic  2. brace  3. invite  4. engaged  5. promise

# You Look Down.

你看起來心情低落。

## Preview 字彙預習

| | |
|---|---|
| accident | 意外；偶然；事故 |
| accuse | 指控；指責；譴責 |
| awful | 糟糕的；慘的 |
| bellow | 吼叫；大聲喝道 |
| care | 在乎；關心；謹慎 |
| cheat | 欺騙 |
| crash | 撞毀 |
| driver's license | 駕照 |
| holler | 大聲喊叫 |
| hopeless | 絕望的；不抱希望的 |
| lousy | 糟糕的；煩躁的 |
| miserable | 痛苦的；悲慘的 |
| reckless | 魯莽的；不顧後果的 |
| roar | 怒吼；呼嘯；喧鬧 |
| scream | 尖叫 |
| shout | 大聲說出；呼喊 |
| signal | 打方向燈；打信號 |
| terrible | 極差的；討厭的 |
| warn | 警告 |
| yell | 吼叫 |

### 行車安全篇

*Karen is in a bad mood when she meets her friend Leon.*

Leon: Why the long face?

Karen: I almost crashed on my way here. A reckless driver changed lanes without signaling.

Leon: Oh my God. You weren't hurt, were you?

Karen: I'm fine. I yelled at the stupid guy, but I doubt he heard me or even cared.

Leon: It's like I always say. They should be more careful about who they give driver's licenses to.

### 翻譯

*凱倫看到她的朋友里昂時,她正處於心情不好的狀態。*

里昂:幹嘛拉長著一張臉?

凱倫:我在來這裡的路上差點**撞車**,有個很**魯莽**的駕駛變換車道時沒打**方向燈**。

里昂:我的天啊,你沒受傷吧?

凱倫:我還好,我對著那個蠢傢伙**大叫**,不過我懷疑他有聽到甚至**注意到**。

里昂:就像我常說的,他們對要發給誰**駕照**應要謹慎一點。

**打電話訴苦篇**

*Stef gives his friend Dorin a call.*

Stef: I just had the worst day ever at work.

Dorin: What happened?

Stef: I gave someone the wrong change by accident. The guy accused me of trying to cheat him. Then my boss warned me not to do it again, like I did it on purpose or something.

Dorin: Man, that's too bad. Do you want to go out for a drink to take your mind off things?

Stef: I guess so. Sorry if I won't be all smiles.

**翻譯**

*史提夫打了個電話給他的朋友朵琳。*

史提夫：我剛度過了工作上最難過的一天。

朵琳　：發生了什麼事？

史提夫：我**無意**中給人找錯了零錢，那個人就**指責**我說我想要**騙**他的錢，然後我老闆就**警告**我別再做那種事，好像我是故意似的。

朵琳　：喔，那真的太糟了。你想去外面喝一杯忘掉那些惱人的事嗎？

史提夫：我想是吧，如果我臉上都沒笑容，在這裡先道歉了。

① **crash** [kræʃ] (*v.*) 撞毀

　例 The road is icy. Slow down or we'll crash.
　　馬路結冰了，慢下來，不然我們會撞車的。

② **reckless** [ˋrɛklɪs] (*adj.*) 不在乎的；魯莽的；不顧後果的

　例 Reckless actions will only get you into trouble.
　　魯莽的行動只會給你招致麻煩。

③ **signal** [ˋsɪgnḷ] (*v.*) 打方向燈；打信號；打暗號

　例 Signal me when it's time to begin.
　　要開始時給我個暗號。

④ **yell** [jɛl] (*v.*) 吼叫

　例 There's no need to yell. I'm standing right next to you.
　　沒必要大聲吼叫吧，我就站在你旁邊啊。

⑤ **care** [kɛr] (*v.*) 在乎；關心；謹慎

　例 If you care about me, you'll help me out.
　　如果你真的關心我，就會幫我這個忙。

⑥ **driver's license** [ˋdraɪvəz ˋlaɪsn̩s] (n.) 駕照

　　例 My driver's license expires in October.
　　我的駕照到十月就到期了。

⑦ **accident** [ˋæksədənt] (n.) 意外；偶然；事故

　　例 I saw a terrible accident on the way to school today.
　　我在去學校的路上，看到一樁很嚴重的事故。

⑧ **accuse** [əˋkjuz] (v.) 指控；指責；譴責

　　例 Don't accuse people of doing something if you don't have any evidence.
　　如果你沒有任何證據，不要隨便指控別人做了某事。

⑨ **cheat** [tʃit] (v.) 欺騙

　　例 The more people you cheat, the more enemies you'll make.
　　你欺騙的人越多，就樹立了越多敵人。

⑩ **warn** [wɔrn] (v.) 警告

　　例 This is the last time I'm going to warn you.
　　這是我最後一次警告你了。

## 🖈 進階字彙

表達過得不好的字

| | | |
|---|---|---|
| **miserable** | [ˋmɪzərəbl] | (adj.) 痛苦的；悲慘的 |
| **awful** | [ˋɔful] | (adj.) 糟糕的；慘的 |
| **hopeless** | [ˋhoplɪs] | (adj.) 絕望的；不抱希望的 |
| **lousy** | [ˋlauzɪ] | (adj.) 糟糕的；煩躁的；差勁的 |
| **terrible** | [ˋtɛrəbl] | (adj.) 極差的；討厭的 |

喊叫的方式

| | | |
|---|---|---|
| **scream** | [skrim] | (v.) 尖叫 |
| **shout** | [ʃaut] | (v.) 大聲說出；呼喊 |
| **holler** | [ˋhɑlə] | (v.) 大聲喊叫 |
| **bellow** | [ˋbɛlo] | (v.) 吼叫；大聲喝道 |
| **roar** | [ror] | (v.) 怒吼；呼嘯；喧鬧 |

文化總匯

美國人年滿十六歲時就可以去考汽車駕照了，考試有分筆試和路考。年輕人通常不會有自己的車，他們會向父母借車，或打工存錢買舊車。有些州規定買車子一定要保險，若發生車禍，看是哪一方的錯，由其保險公司負責理賠，若肇事車沒有保險，不僅要賠償損失，還會被告。

# ✎ Exercises 動手做

請從以下字彙中，挑出正確的單字填入空格內。

| reckless | accident | signal | |
|----------|----------|--------|------|
| yelling | cheated | accuse | care |

1. I didn't _____ you of anything. I only asked if you did it.

2. Slow down, or we'll get into an _____.

3. The way you're _____, everyone in the building can hear you.

4. The careless factory worker was _____ in the way he did his job.

5. There are a lot of dishonest merchants in that market. Be careful you don't get _____ by them.

1. 我沒有指控你任何事，我只是問是不是你做的。

2. 慢一點，不然我們會發生意外。

3. 你大叫的樣子，整棟大樓裡的人都聽到了。

4. 那個心不在焉的員工對他自己工作的方式毫不在乎。

5. 那個市場裡有很多不誠實的商家，你要小心不要被他們騙了。

解答 1. accuse  2. accident  3. yelling  4. reckless  5. cheated

# Should We Tell Everyone?

我們該告訴大家嗎？

## Preview 字彙預習

| | |
|---|---|
| **autumn** | 秋季 |
| **cautious** | 十分小心謹慎的 |
| **clandestine** | 暗中做下的 |
| **concerned** | 擔心的；在意的 |
| **couple** | 一對情侶（夫婦） |
| **fall** | 秋天 |
| **harm** | 傷害 |
| **hidden** | 隱密的；隱藏的 |
| **immoral** | 不道德的；傷風敗俗的 |
| **interfere** | 妨礙；干涉；介入 |
| **paranoid** | 神經質的 |
| **practical** | 實際的；現實的 |
| **satisfied** | 滿意的；心滿意足的 |
| **secretive** | 偷偷摸摸的 |
| **sneaky** | 鬼鬼祟祟的；躡手躡腳的 |
| **spring** | 春天 |
| **summer** | 夏天 |
| **unknown** | 未知的；沒人知道的 |
| **vacation** | 假期 |
| **winter** | 冬天 |

夏日戀情篇

*It's the end of summer vacation. Pete and Connie have been spending a lot of time together.*

Pete: Vacation went by so fast.

Connie: It always does. Are we still going to see each other when school starts?

Pete: Sure, why not?

Connie: Then that means we have to tell everyone we're a couple.

Pete: If you want. I'm not concerned about what other people think. As long as we're happy, then I'm satisfied.

翻譯

*暑假就快結束了，比特和康妮花了很多時間相處。*

比特：**假期**過得好快。

康妮：放假都是這樣的。開學後我們還會繼續交往嗎？

比特：當然會啊，為什麼不？

康妮：那麼，那就表示我們必須告訴大家我們是**男女朋友**。

比特：看你啊，我是**不在乎**別人怎麼想啦，只要我們開心，我就**心滿意足**了。

## 辦公室戀情

*Raymond and Mary Joe work at the same company. They've been going out for a few months.*

Mary Joe: Raymond, why do we have to be so secretive at work? It's not like we're doing anything wrong or immoral.

Raymond: Of course we're not. But, I don't want anyone there to interfere in our lives.

Mary Joe: Isn't that being paranoid? What could any of our colleagues possibly do to harm us?

Raymond: For starters, they could gossip, or ask personal questions. I don't know. I'm just trying to be practical. I don't want anything or anyone to come between us.

Mary Joe: I won't let that happen.

## 翻譯

*雷蒙和瑪莉嬌在同一個公司上班，他們已經約會幾個月了。*

瑪莉嬌：雷蒙，我們上班時為什麼一定要這麼**偷偷摸摸**的？我們又不是在做壞事或什麼**不道德的**事。

雷蒙　：我們當然不是，我只是不想讓任何人來**干擾**我們的生活。

瑪莉嬌：你會不會太**神經質**？我們的同事中哪有什麼人可能做什麼事來**傷害**我們？

雷蒙　：對剛在一起的人來說，他們可能會八卦一下或問些私人問題。我不曉得啦，我只是想**實際**一點，我不想讓任何事或任何人破壞我們。

瑪莉嬌：我不會讓那種事發生的。

① **vacation** [veˋkeʃən] (*n.*) 假期

例 What do you plan to do during winter vacation?
你寒假時打算做什麼？

② **couple** [ˋkʌpl̩] (*n.*) 一對情侶（夫婦）

例 You two make an adorable couple.
你們兩個是很可愛的一對。

③ **concerned** [kənˋsɝnd] (*adj.*) 擔心的；在意的

例 I still don't see why you're concerned about his opinion.
我實在不了解你為什麼在意他的意見。

④ **satisfied** [ˋsætɪsˏfaɪd] (*adj.*) 滿意的；心滿意足的

例 One thing about Ben, he's never satisfied.
班特別的一點就是他從來不滿足。

⑤ **secretive** [sɪˋkritɪv] (*adj.*) 隱隱藏藏的；偷偷摸摸的

例 This is all so secretive. I feel like I'm in a spy movie.
這一切都這麼神秘，我覺得自己好像在演諜報片。

⑥ **immoral** [ɪˋmɔrəl] (*adj.*) 不道德的；傷風敗俗的

例 I don't approve of what Miranda did, but I don't think it was immoral.

雖然我不認同米蘭達所做的事，不過我倒不覺得那有什麼不道德的。

⑦ **interfere** [ˌɪntəˋfɪr] (*v.*) 妨礙；干涉；介入

例 I hope you don't think I'm interfering in your business.

我希望你不要認為我在干預你的事。

⑧ **paranoid** [ˋpærəˌnɔɪd] (*adj.*) 神經質的

例 It's all right to be cautious, as long as you're not paranoid.

小心點是好的，只要不太過神經質。

⑨ **harm** [hɑrm] (*v.*) 傷害

例 Keeping that kind of thing secret could harm your relationship.

連那種事都保密會傷害到你們之間的關係的。

⑩ **practical** [ˋpræktɪkl] (*adj.*) 實際的；現實的

例 Why do we have to be practical all the time?

我們為什麼總是要這麼實際？

## 📌 進階字彙

### 四季

| | | |
|---|---|---|
| **summer** | [ˋsʌmɚ] (*n.*) | 夏天 |
| **fall** | [fɔl] (*n.*) | 秋天 |
| **autumn** | [ˋɔtəm] (*n.*) | 秋季 |
| **spring** | [sprɪŋ] (*n.*) | 春天 |
| **winter** | [ˋwɪntɚ] (*n.*) | 冬天 |

### 描述偷偷摸摸的舉動

| | | |
|---|---|---|
| **sneaky** | [ˋsnikɪ] (*adj.*) | 鬼鬼祟祟的；躡手躡腳的 |
| **clandestine** | [klænˋdɛstɪn] (*adj.*) | 暗中做下的 |
| **cautious** | [ˋkɔʃəs] (*adj.*) | 十分小心謹慎的 |
| **unknown** | [ʌnˋnon] (*adj.*) | 未知的；沒人知道的 |
| **hidden** | [ˋhɪdṇ] (*adj.*) | 隱密的；隱藏的 |

文化總匯

在美國，國小、國中、高中的假期時段都差不多一樣：暑假從六月底開始到九月初結束，有兩個月的時間；寒假配合耶誕假期與新年，從十二月中旬開始，到一月上旬結束，大概都有三個禮拜的時間；春假則是一個星期，時間是在四月份。

# ✎ Exercises 動手做

請從以下字彙中，挑出正確的單字填入空格內。

| vacation | concerned | practical | |
|----------|-----------|-----------|------|
| couple | satisfied | interferes | harm |

1. Seth frequently _____ in matters that have nothing to do with him.

2. If you're not _____ with your present situation, then do something to change it.

3. I'm so excited. Summer _____ starts in five days!

4. Jane and Philip were voted the most attractive _____ at the dance.

5. It is a beautiful house, but I don't think living this far from work is very _____.

1. 席斯經常干涉與他毫不相關的事。
2. 如果你不滿現狀，就做些事去改變它。
3. 我好高興，再五天就要開始放暑假了。
4. 珍和菲力普在舞會中被票選為最吸引人的一對。
5. 這房子很漂亮，不過住在離工作這麼遠的地方恐怕有點不切實際。

解答  1. interferes   2. satisfied   3. vacation   4. couple   5. practical

## Preview 字彙預習

| | |
|---|---|
| **angry** | 氣憤的 |
| **basement** | 地下室 |
| **civil** | 文明的；客氣的 |
| **comic book** | 漫畫書 |
| **contradict** | 反駁；與……矛盾 |
| **enraged** | 激憤的 |
| **finances** | 經濟；財務 |
| **furious** | 狂怒的 |
| **hurry** | 趕緊；快點 |
| **junk** | 垃圾 |
| **livid** | 非常生氣的 |
| **mad** | 生氣的 |
| **maniac** | 瘋子 |
| **possessions** | 財產；擁有物 |
| **relationships** | 關係 |
| **reputations** | 名望；名譽 |
| **responsibilities** | 責任 |
| **sarcastic** | 挖苦的；諷刺的；尖刻的 |
| **speed** | 超速 |
| **valuable** | 值錢的；貴重的 |

**開車篇**

*Albert and Wendy are on their way to a movie. They're running late.*

Wendy: Slow down. You're driving like a maniac.

Albert: Do you want to get there on time or not? First you want me to hurry, now you want me to slow down. Stop contradicting yourself.

Wendy: I didn't mean you should speed. And you don't have to be sarcastic.

Albert: Look, I.... Wendy, We're almost there. Let's try to be civil. I'll turn on the radio.

Wendy: Fine with me.

**翻譯**

*亞伯特和溫蒂正在往電影院的路上，他們快遲到了。*

溫蒂 ：開慢一點，你開車像個**瘋子**似的。

亞伯特：妳到底想不想準時到那裡啊？妳先要我開**快點**，現在又要我慢下來，別再自我**矛盾**了。

溫蒂 ：我不是說你得**超速**，而且，你也不必**挖苦**我吧。

亞伯特：聽著，我……。溫蒂，我們就快到了，試著**文明**點吧，我來開收音機。

溫蒂 ：隨便你，我無所謂。

晚餐篇

*Cindy and Matt are having dinner at a restaurant.*

Cindy: I found a couple of boxes of comic books when I was cleaning the basement. They seemed pretty old, so I threw them away.

Matt: You did what? Do you have any idea how valuable those are? I can't believe this!

Cindy: The truth is, we need space. The house is full of your junk as it is.

Matt: Who cares about space? Those were my personal things.

Cindy: Calm down. I put the boxes next to the garbage cans outside. They're probably still there. We'll check when we get home.

翻譯

*辛蒂和麥特正在一家餐館裡用晚餐。*

辛蒂：我在清理**地下室**時，發現了幾箱**漫畫書**，它們看起來都很舊，所以我就把它們丟了。

麥特：妳做了什麼事？妳知不知道那些漫畫書有多**貴重**啊？我真是無法相信！

辛蒂：事實上是，我們需要空間，房子裡已經塞滿你那些**垃圾**了。

麥特：誰在乎空間啊？那些是我的私人物品。

辛蒂：冷靜下來，我把箱子放在我們家外面的垃圾筒旁邊，它們應該還在原地，我們回家時再看一下。

① **maniac** [ˋmenɪˌæk] (n.) 瘋子

例 Stop waving your arms around like a maniac.
別像個瘋子似的揮舞你的手臂。

---

② **hurry** [ˋhɝɪ] (v.) 趕緊；快點

例 Take your time. There's no reason to hurry.
慢慢來，沒有理由要那麼急。

---

③ **contradict** [ˌkɑntrəˋdɪkt] (v.) 反駁；與……矛盾

例 The politician contradicted his opponent whenever he got the chance.
這個政客只要一有機會就會反駁他的對手。

---

④ **speed** [spid] (v.) 超速

例 I'm sure the driver who hit me was speeding.
我很確定撞到我的那個駕駛他超速。

---

⑤ **sarcastic** [sɑrˋkæstɪk] (adj.) 挖苦的；諷刺的；尖刻的

例 That was a very sarcastic thing to say.
那說來很諷刺。

6 **civil** [`sɪvl] (*adj.*) 文明的；客氣的

例 When we talk to Professor Daniels, remember to be civil and courteous.
我們等一下跟丹尼爾斯教授說話時，記得要客氣有禮貌。

7 **comic book** [`kɑmɪk `buk] (*n.*) 漫畫書

例 What comic books did you read when you were a kid?
你小時候都看什麼樣的漫畫書？

8 **basement** [`besmənt] (*n.*) 地下室

例 The basement was flooded after the heavy rains.
下大雨之後，地下室淹水了。

9 **valuable** [`væljəbl] (*adj.*) 值錢的；貴重的

例 The store owner displayed his most valuable items in a glass case.
店家把他最值錢的物品放在玻璃櫃裡展示。

10 **junk** [dʒʌŋk] (*n.*) 垃圾

例 Why did you buy all that junk at the flea market?
你幹嘛在跳蚤市場買那些垃圾？

### 人們所爭吵的事情

| | |
|---|---|
| **finances** | [faɪˋnænsɪz] (*n.*) 經濟；財務 |
| **relationships** | [rɪˋleʃənʃɪps] (*n.*) 關係 |
| **possessions** | [pəˋzɛʃənz] (*n.*) 財產；擁有物 |
| **reputations** | [ˏrɛpjəˋteʃənz] (*n.*) 名望；名譽 |
| **responsibilities** | [rɪˏspɑnsəˋbɪlətɪz] (*n.*) 責任 |

### 表達生氣的字

| | |
|---|---|
| **mad** | [mæd] (*adj.*) 生氣的 |
| **angry** | [ˋæŋgrɪ] (*adj.*) 氣憤的 |
| **furious** | [ˋfjurɪəs] (*adj.*) 狂怒的 |
| **livid** | [ˋlɪvɪd] (*adj.*) 非常生氣的 |
| **enraged** | [ɪnˋredʒd] (*adj.*) 激憤的 |

文化總匯

在美國，很多人會收集漫畫書、玩具、棒球卡等等各式各類的收藏，很多這類的東西，只要年代一久遠，就會變得很值錢，不過也要看物品的狀態如何，物品狀態好的，甚至連外包裝都未被拆封過的，會是最值錢的，若物體有破損、刮傷等等，當然價值就會比較低了。

# ✏ Exercises 動手做

請從以下字彙中，挑出正確的單字填入空格內。

| contradict | comic book | valuable | |
|------------|------------|----------|------|
| maniac | Hurry | speed | junk |

1. _____, we only have twenty minutes to catch the train.

2. This coin is the most _____ piece in my collection.

3. Don't _____, or you're going to get pulled over by a policeman.

4. That guy's a _____. I asked him a simple question, and he started yelling at me for no reason.

5. Can I read that _____ when you're done with it?

1. 快點，我們只有二十分鐘可以趕火車。
2. 這硬幣是我收藏裡最值錢的一枚。
3. 別超速，不然你會被警察攔下來的。
4. 那傢伙是個瘋子，我只是問他個簡單的問題，他就開始毫無理由地對我大叫。
5. 你看完那本漫畫後，可以給我看嗎？

解答 1. Hurry  2. valuable  3. speed  4. maniac  5. comic book

**A** 選一最適合的字完成下列句子

1. John was very _____ about his new work project and wouldn't tell anyone about it.
   A) concerned              B) paranoid
   C) sarcastic              D) secretive

2. Jessica's _____ is in sales, but she's also interested in marketing.
   A) promise                B) background
   C) coincidence            D) exception

3. Although _____ often have glamorous lifestyles, they also have to deal with a lack of privacy and other problems.
   A) celebrities            B) accidents
   C) maniacs                D) vacations

4. Since it was so loud in the restaurant, Monica had to _____ to get the waiter's attention.
   A) warn                   B) hint
   C) yell                   D) invite

5. Joe and Lisa have been _____ for two years, and their friends are wondering if they'll ever get married.
   A) satisfied              B) practical
   C) exhausting             D) engaged

**B** 將下列空格填入最適合的單字

Investing in the stock market isn't as easy as it used to be. Stocks have never been guaranteed investments, but 10-20 years ago, they were far more stable than they are now (with some ___(1)___, of course). These days, markets are sensitive to a variety of news reports, including political news, economic news, and even weather reports. The ___(2)___ of investors can quickly change, as indexes might rise or fall 2-3 percent based on a good or bad news story, even if the story is only related to a small segment of the market.

Analysts say people should be cautious when investing in stocks. They ___(3)___ people against being ___(4)___ and investing in too many risky companies. Instead, it's important to diversify one's portfolio, with holdings in large and small firms. Above all, analysts remind us that stocks are long-term investments, and people shouldn't be in a ___(5)___ to see a big return on their stock investments.

1. (A) signals     (B) ultrasounds (C) exceptions   (D) backgrounds
2. (A) mood       (B) accident    (C) coincidence (D) junk
3. (A) inspect     (B) bother      (C) accuse      (D) warn
4. (A) romantic   (B) concerned   (C) valuable     (D) reckless
5. (A) hurry       (B) speed       (C) maniac       (D) harm

**A** 1. D　2. B　3. A　4. C　5. D

翻譯

1. 約翰對他的新工作專案很保密，不告訴任何人。
2. 潔西卡的背景是在銷售方面，但她對行銷也有興趣。
3. 雖然名流常有迷人的生活方式，但是他們也必須應付缺乏隱私權以及其他的問題。
4. 由於餐廳裡面是如此的喧鬧，莫妮卡必須要喊叫才能引起服務生的注意。
5. 喬和麗莎已經訂婚兩年了，而他們的朋友很好奇他們到底會不會結婚。

**B** 1. C　2. A　3. D　4. D　5. A

翻譯

投資股票市場不再像以前那麼容易。股票從來都不是有保障的投資，但是十到二十年以前，它們可是比現在穩定的多了（當然，也有一些例外）。現今，市場對種種新聞報導很敏感，包括政治新聞、財經新聞、甚至是氣象報告。投資人的情緒可以變化地很快，就像指數會隨著一則好消息或壞消息上升或下跌二到三個百分點，即使那則報導只跟市場的一小部份有關係而已。

分析師指出大家投資股票市場時應該小心謹慎。他們警告大家不要魯莽，並且投資風險太高的公司。反之，分散投資是很重要的，持有的股票應包含大、小型的公司。最重要的是，分析師提醒我們股票是長期的投資，而且大家不該急著要見到股票投資有大筆的收益。

# 學習字彙的正確方法

死記大量的單字，遠不如真正學會使用幾個核心字彙！

## ☑ 從情境對話中學習字彙，更能掌握如何使用字彙！

上下文情境對於理解他人的話是非常重要的。字彙與片語通常是句子的組成元素，也是某種場合情境中人們對話的一部份。這是真實生活中語言被使用的情形，能運用此一概念來學習字彙就顯得非常重要，也就是運用上下文情境來學習。而這也是為何本書用各種情境對話來呈現字彙的原因。這樣的方式非但讓我們認識在特定情境下該如何使用字彙，也能使我們了解人與字彙互動的方式。這是許多字彙書沒有注意到的，它們只是將字彙用句子呈現出來，雖是有用但仍不足夠。

## ☑ 從不同的面向、不同的例子來學習一個單字

如果要瞭解如何使用字彙或片語，只讀一個例子是不夠的。多種不同的上下文能提供豐富又有變化的例句，也能給學習者更多的自信，以及對所學字彙有更深入的了解。這本書從「Andrew's 精選對話」、「核心字彙」到「Exercises 動手做」提供了多種情境作為單字的使用背景，提升讀者對單字使用的熟悉度。

## ☑ 聽讀同步

研讀本書時，請務必搭配 MP3，這是訓練聽力的絕佳機會。在讀完「Andrew's 精選對話」後，請聽 MP3 練習。第一次聽的時候，請對照著書。第二次時，請把書闔上，專心聽就好，聽聽句子的語調、

以及字彙與字彙銜接後的念法。當你花時間聽了 MP3 中生動的口語對話後，你就更能理解英語母語人士他們運用字彙的方式。

## ☑ 練習

一旦你學會了如何用自然生動的英語來呈現字彙後，此時，能藉由練習來測試一下學習成果就很重要。本書提供了簡易的練習，包含「Exercises 動手做」、「單字總複習」等單元，來幫助讀者記憶所學的字彙。這些練習全都是非常道地、自然且口語的英文。

# 複習單字的正確方法

複習是英文學習中重要的一環，但卻最容易被忽略。無論你正在學習的是購物所須的單字、或者是旅遊時所須的句子、還是在飛機上的措詞表達，經常性地複習你所學過的東西是一件重要的事。

### 複習法則 1　不斷回頭檢視前面所學，並列出清單。

通常，語言學習者都盡可能的想在短時間內看完很多單字及句型。這當然是個值得鼓勵的目標，不過學習語言並不像是搭高鐵一樣高速直駛就能到站，而是必須養成一種固定的學習模式，並在學習新的字彙或片語後，不斷的回頭複習前面所學。

在在本書中，我建議一次先讀個四到五個單元，再從頭複習一遍。重新讀一次對話並且看看還記得多少，如果可以的話，甚至還可將

所學的字列一張清單，每天看一遍。在開始新單元之前，檢視自己在前一天或是上個星期，甚至是上個月所學的字彙，如果還能充分掌握這些字彙，你就可以在清單上將這些字畫掉，然後把注意力集中到覺得較難的單字。

書中在每個章節最後，都有一個複習的單元，包含了數個練習來幫助你們複習在各章節中所學的字。倘若你能無誤地完成習題，就表示你已經準備好進行下個章節了。如果還不行，我建議還是再回去看看是對那些字的用法不熟悉。

**複習法則 2** **透過自己生產的句子，強化對單字的認識。**

目前，我已經嚐過學習六種語言的樂趣。是哪幾種語言呢？讓我來告訴那些有興趣想知道的人，中文、日文、西班牙文、法文、德文以及英文。有些我可以說的很好，有些則只是在基礎階段。大部分的原因還是歸於所花時間的多寡，以及練習的次數。總之，對所學過的每一種語言，我都養成了一個習慣，就是寫句子。

我會用本子記下學到的新字彙。也會依照俚語、成語、或其他特殊的語言型態來將我的筆記分門別類。像是單字或片語就寫在頁面的左邊，然後接著寫下詞性，再來是解釋。同一行（若還有空間，若沒有就寫在下一行）我會寫下我所造的句子，不需是很複雜的句子，只是要能證明自己會用這個字，重要的是我不是從書上抄的。任何人都會抄的，不過，將自己的句子寫下來能夠增強我對單字或片語的認識，並且使我能更主動的去學習。

我每天基本上都會把清單複習一遍。為了要測驗自己的學習成果，我會把解釋的地方先折起來，然後看自己是否理解所列出的單字和片語。接下來，我會在頁面上空白處用那些單字寫下句子。如果列出的單字很多，我就會選擇幾個來造句。句子可長可短，可以是嚴肅也可以是有趣的，也可以是有關任何主題的。我每天都會花上至少二十到三十分鐘作練習，因為我認為這是學習語言中最為重要的層面。如果你沒那麼多時間，五到十分鐘也可以，在公車、捷運或是當你在吃早餐時寫下一些句子。重要的是養成習慣。你就會發現自己寫下了生活中各種有趣的事，那些發生在工作上，或新聞上的事。最令人興奮的是，你可是用英文寫的喔！

# Chapter 2
# 人際關係

英語學習專欄 **2**

該學哪些字彙呢？

## Preview 字彙預習

| | |
|---|---|
| **anticipate** | 預期；預料 |
| **apologize** | 道歉；認錯 |
| **argue** | 爭吵；爭論；吵架 |
| **blame** | 責怪 |
| **borrow** | 借用 |
| **careful** | 小心的；仔細的 |
| **cause** | 原因；動機 |
| **cry** | 哭；喊叫 |
| **fault** | 過錯；責任 |
| **forgive** | 原諒；寬恕 |
| **frown** | 皺眉頭 |
| **horrible** | 糟糕的；恐怖的 |
| **narrow** | 狹窄的 |
| **reason** | 原因；理由 |
| **right** | 對的 |
| **scratch** | 刮傷；擦傷 |
| **traffic** | 交通狀況 |
| **trust** | 信任；相信 |
| **upset** | 心煩的；不高興的 |
| **wrong** | 錯的 |

**擦傷朋友的車篇**

*Wendy damaged Neil's car while driving it.*

Neil:     I can't believe you scratched my car. You said you'd be careful if I let you borrow it.

Wendy:    But, I was. The street was narrow, and there wasn't much space to drive through. I'm really sorry.

Neil:     God, I was stupid to trust you. It's going to take me months to save up for a new paint job.

Wendy:    I'll help you pay.

Neil:     I hope so.

**翻譯**

*溫蒂駕駛尼爾的車時損壞了它。*

尼爾：我無法相信妳竟**擦傷**了我的車，妳說過如果我讓妳**借用**我的車，妳會小心的。

溫蒂：我是很小心啊，那個巷道很**窄**，而且也沒有足夠的空間可以開過去，我真的很抱歉。

尼爾：老天爺，我真的太笨了才會**相信**妳，我要花好幾個月的時間才能存夠重新烤漆的錢。

溫蒂：我會幫忙付的。

尼爾：希望如此。

男伴遲到篇

*Shelly's date arrives an hour late.*

Shelly: So, you decided to come. Go ahead, I'm listening...

Isaac: Please don't be upset. Traffic was very heavy on the way here.

Shelly: What time did you leave your house?

Isaac: About 5:45. I didn't anticipate such horrible traffic. I do apologize.

Shelly: Well, anyway, let's order. You look about as hungry as I am.

翻譯

*雪莉的男伴晚了一個小時才到。*

雪莉　：你終於決定出現啦，說吧，我在聽…

艾薩克：拜託別**生氣**，到這裡的路上**交通**非常壅塞。

雪莉　：你幾點出門的？

艾薩克：大概五點四十五，我沒**預期**交通狀況會這麼**糟糕**，我真的很**抱歉**。

雪莉　：不管怎樣，我們還是先點菜吧，你看起來就跟我一樣餓。

① **scratch** [skrætʃ] (v.) 刮傷；擦傷

> 例 Try not to scratch the TV as you carry it in.
>
> 你搬電視進來時，盡量別刮傷它。

② **careful** [`kɛrfəl] (adj.) 小心的；仔細的

> 例 I promise I'll be careful.
>
> 我保證我會小心的。

③ **borrow** [`baro] (v.) 借用

> 例 How much do you need to borrow?
>
> 你需要借多少錢？

④ **narrow** [`næro] (adj.) 狹窄的

> 例 They had trouble pushing the cart down the narrow alley.
>
> 他們要在狹窄的巷道裡推過推車有些麻煩。

⑤ **trust** [trʌst] (v.) 信任；相信

> 例 After what happened, I don't know if I can trust you anymore.
>
> 在發生了那些事後，我不知道我是不是還能再相信你。

⑥ **upset** [ʌp`sɛt] (*adj.*) 心煩的；不高興的

例 Emma was clearly upset when I saw her.
我看到艾瑪時，她很明顯地心情不佳。

⑦ **traffic** [`træfɪk] (*n.*) 交通狀況

例 Is there any way around this traffic?
有沒有任何路可以繞過這裡的交通狀況？

⑧ **anticipate** [æn`tɪsə ,pet] (*v.*) 預期；預料

例 We should have anticipated something like this happening.
我們早該料到會發生這種事的。

⑨ **horrible** [`hɔrəbl̩] (*adj.*) 糟糕的；恐怖的

例 That restaurant is truly horrible.
那家餐廳真的很糟糕。

⑩ **apologize** [ə`pɑlə ,dʒaɪz] (*v.*) 道歉；認錯；賠不是

例 I've already apologized, and I'm not going to do it again.
我已經道過歉了，而且我不會再那樣做了。

## 📌 進階字彙

### 藉口的相關用字

| | | |
|---|---|---|
| **reason** | [ˋrizṇ] (*n.*) | 原因;理由 |
| **cause** | [kɔz] (*n.*) | 原因;動機 |
| **fault** | [fɔlt] (*n.*) | 過錯;責任 |
| **right** | [raɪt] (*adj.*) | 對的 |
| **wrong** | [rɔŋ] (*adj.*) | 錯的 |

### 對藉口的反應

| | | |
|---|---|---|
| **forgive** | [fɚˋgɪv] (*v.*) | 原諒;寬恕 |
| **blame** | [blem] (*v.*) | 責怪 |
| **argue** | [ˋɑrgju] (*v.*) | 爭吵;爭論;吵架 |
| **cry** | [kraɪ] (*v.*) | 哭;喊叫 |
| **frown** | [fraun] (*v.*) | 皺眉頭 |

文化總匯

美國文化裡,借東西的雙方都有一定的共識:甲如果向乙借東西,在借用期間,如果東西有所損壞,甲必須向乙道歉並且負責賠償,賠償的方法有兩種,一種是金錢理賠,另一種是買一個新的還給乙。

# ✎ Exercises 動手做

請從以下字彙中，挑出正確的單字填入空格內。

| apologize | anticipate | scratch | |
|-----------|------------|---------|------|
| upset | traffic | narrow | trust |

1. The radio said _____ on that road is very heavy.

2. I didn't do anything wrong, so I don't think I should _____.

3. Don't cry. Tell me what you're _____ about.

4. That _____ on the table was there when I bought it.

5. It's important to be able to _____ our friends.

1. 廣播說那條路的交通很壅塞。
2. 我沒做錯什麼，所以我覺得我不需要道歉。
3. 別哭，告訴我妳在煩些什麼？
4. 我買那個桌子時，那條刮痕早就在上面了。
5. 能信任我們的朋友是很重要的事。

解答 1. traffic　2. apologize　3. upset　4. scratch　5. trust

# What A Nice Outfit!

你打扮得好漂亮！

## Preview 字彙預習

| | |
|---|---|
| ball | 舞會 |
| birthday party | 慶生聚會 |
| black tie | 半正式的 |
| casual | 不拘禮節的、非正式的 |
| chase | 追逐；追求；追擊 |
| compliment | 讚美；恭維 |
| costume party | 戲服裝扮舞會 |
| date | 約會的對象；約會 |
| embarrass | 使難堪；使不好意思 |
| escort | 陪同；護送；護航 |
| formal | 正式的 |
| going away party | 惜別聚會 |
| gown | 禮服 |
| informal | 非正式的 |
| masquerade | 化妝舞會（戴面具） |
| party | 舞會；聚會 |
| proud | 驕傲的；得意的；有自尊心的 |
| rowdy | 喧嚷的；吵鬧的 |
| serious | 認真嚴肅的 |
| striking | 迷倒眾生的；驚人的 |

**晚會聚餐篇**

*Cheryl has spent the last hour getting ready for a formal dinner party.*

Paul: Look out, Manhattan! You are simply striking in that gown.

Cheryl: Thank you. That's what I like—a good compliment to start the evening.

Paul: I'll be the luckiest guy at the party.

Cheryl: Hey, slow down. Don't use up all your compliments so fast. We haven't even left yet.

Paul: I'm just telling the truth. Can't a guy be proud of having a beautiful date?

**翻譯**

*雪柔正為赴一個正式的晚餐聚會做最後一小時的準備。*

保羅：妳看外面，曼哈頓耶！那件**禮服**穿在妳身上簡直就是**美極**了。

雪柔：謝謝，那正是我喜歡的──以一個好的**讚美**作為這個晚上的開始。

保羅：我將會是宴會裡最幸運的傢伙。

雪柔：嘿，慢慢來，別這麼快就用完你的讚美，我們甚至還沒離開呢。

保羅：我說的是實話，難道一個男人不能為他美麗的**女伴**感到**驕傲**嗎？

*Philip is about to go out on his first date.*

Philip: Mom, what time is it?

Mother: 6:20. Don't you look nice. All the girls will be chasing you around.

Philip: Aw, come on, I'm just going to a movie. Lisa should be here soon. Please don't embarrass me in front of her.

Mother: I won't. Are you sure you don't want me to escort you two?

Philip: That's not even funny. Please tell me you're not serious.

翻譯

*菲力普就要出門赴第一次約會。*

菲力普：媽，現在幾點了？

母親　：六點二十分。你看起來真帥，所有的女孩都會追著你跑。

菲力普：喔，拜託，我只是去看電影而已，莉莎應該快到這裡了，請別在她面前糗我。

母親　：我不會啦，你確定你不想要我幫你們兩個護航嗎？

菲力普：一點都不好笑，請告訴我你不是認真的。

① **striking** [ˋstraɪkɪŋ] (*adj.*) 迷倒眾生的；驚人的

例 What a striking necklace she's wearing.
她戴的那條項鍊好顯目。

② **gown** [ɡaʊn] (*n.*) 禮服

例 The seamstress said my gown will be ready by tomorrow.
女裁縫師說我的禮服明天就會準備好了。

③ **compliment** [ˋkɑmpləmənt] (*n.*) 讚美；恭維

例 Marsha loves receiving compliments.
瑪莎很喜歡接受別人的恭維。

④ **party** [ˋpɑrtɪ] (*n.*) 舞會；聚會

例 Call Gary for directions to the party.
打電話問蓋瑞舞會要怎麼到。

⑤ **proud** [praʊd] (*adj.*) 驕傲的；得意的；有自尊心的

例 Nina doesn't like boys who are too proud.
妮娜不喜歡太驕傲的男孩子。

6. **date** [det] (*n.*) 約會的對象；男／女伴；約會

例 Now, sit down, have some tea, and tell me all about your date.

現在，坐下來，喝些茶，然後告訴我所有跟你約會有關的事。

7. **chase** [tʃes] (*v.*) 追逐；追求；追擊

例 That stupid dog chases my car every time I drive by.

每次我開車經過時，那隻笨狗都追著我跑。

8. **embarrass** [ɪmˋbærəs] (*v.*) 使難堪；使不好意思

例 Kurt likes to embarrass his brother whenever he gets the chance.

柯特只要一有機會就喜歡糗他老弟。

9. **escort** [ˋɛskɔrt] (*v.*) 陪同；護送；護航

例 The group of school children was escorted to the park by several teachers.

這群學生由幾個老師陪同到公園裡去。

10. **serious** [ˋsɪrɪəs] (*adj.*) 認真嚴肅的；不是開玩笑的

例 Try to have a good time. Don't look so serious.

盡量玩得開心點，別這麼嚴肅。

## 🖋 進階字彙

**masquerade**      [ˌmæskəˋred] (n.) 化妝舞會（戴面具）

**costume party**      [ˋkɑstjum ˋpɑrtɪ] (n.) 戲服裝扮舞會

**ball**      [bɔl] (n.) 舞會

**birthday party**      [ˋbɝθˌde ˋpɑrtɪ] (n.) 慶生聚會

**going away party**      [ˋgoɪŋ əˋwe ˋpɑrtɪ] (n.) 惜別聚會

形容宴會

**formal**      [ˋfɔrml] (adj.) 正式的

**informal**      [ɪnˋfɔrml] (adj.) 非正式的

**casual**      [ˋkæʒuəl] (adj.) 不拘禮節的、非正式的

**rowdy**      [ˋraʊdɪ] (adj.) 喧嘩的；吵鬧的

**black tie**      [ˋblæk ˋtaɪ] (adj.) 半正式的

文化總匯

美國的小孩通常在青少年時期就開始交男女朋友，當他們開始約會時，都不喜歡父母陪他們一起去，所以父母都會規定他們在規定的時間內回到家，如果他們是晚上出去約會，國中生大概需在九點、十點左右回家，而高中生就大概得在十一點、十二點前回到家。

# Exercises 動手做

請從以下字彙中，挑出正確的單字填入空格內。

| embarrass | striking | compliment | |
| proud | date | chase | gown |

1. Mr. Nickels was _____ of his son's accomplishments.

2. That chicken is in our yard again. Can you _____ it away?

3. The actress, wearing an expensive _____, walked into the room like a queen.

4. Al is going to be my _____ to the party.

5. I'm sure a lot of people will _____ you on your beautiful outfit.

1. 尼可斯先生對他兒子的成就引以為傲。
2. 那隻雞又跑到我們院子裡,你能趕走它嗎?
3. 那個女演員穿了件昂貴的禮服,像個皇后似的走進房間。
4. 艾爾會是我去舞會時的男伴。
5. 我相信會有很多人讚美你美麗的穿著。

解答 1. proud  2. chase  3. gown  4. date  5. compliment

## Preview 字彙預習

| | |
|---|---|
| **affair** | 婚外情；外遇 |
| **apartment** | 公寓 |
| **betray** | 背叛 |
| **conceal** | 隱瞞 |
| **condominium** | 分戶出售的公寓 |
| **disloyal** | 不忠實的；不忠誠的 |
| **extreme** | 極端的；偏激的 |
| **flat** | 一層樓房 |
| **gigantic** | 巨大的；龐大的 |
| **house** | 房子 |
| **imbecile** | 低能者；傻子 |
| **kiss** | 親吻 |
| **liar** | 騙子 |
| **move** | 搬動；搬家 |
| **original** | 最初的；原本的 |
| **penthouse** | 建築物頂層的豪華公寓 |
| **rent** | 租 |
| **secret** | 秘密 |
| **suite** | 套房 |
| **whisper** | 耳語；私語 |

# Andrew's 精選對話

男友出軌篇

*Nicole has discovered her boyfriend was unfaithful to her.*

Nicole: I couldn't believe it when I saw you kissing Dorin Kirby by the library.

Chad: I wasn't kissing her. I just whispered something to her.

Nicole: Oh, you are such a gigantic liar. Do you think I'm an imbecile or something?

Chad: Nicole, you're the only one for me.

Nicole: Like I really believe that. That's probably what you "whispered" to Dorin, isn't it?

翻譯

*妮可發現她的男友對她不忠實。*

妮可：我看到你在圖書館旁**親**朵琳‧柯比的時候，我簡直不能相信。

查得：我不是在親她，我只是在跟她講**悄悄話**。

妮可：喔，你真是個**大騙子**，你覺得我是**智障**或是什麼的嗎？

查得：妮可，妳是我的唯一啊。

妮可：你講得好像我會相信一樣。你大概也是這麼對朵琳「耳語」的吧，對吧？

分手篇

*Luke gives his girlfriend a call.*

Luke: Um, Betty, you know my parents are moving to Texas, right?

Betty: Yeah, and you're going to rent an apartment here, in Cincinnati.

Luke: That was my original plan. Now, I've decided to go with my parents. I think maybe you and I should stop seeing each other.

Betty: Isn't that kind of extreme? I could still come visit you.

Luke: Well, maybe. We could give it a try for a while.

翻譯

*路克打電話給他的女友。*

路克：嗯，貝蒂，妳知道我爸媽要**搬**到德州去，對吧？

貝蒂：是啊，而你要在辛辛那堤這裡**租個公寓**。

路克：那是我**原本**的計劃，現在，我決定跟我的父母一起去，我想也許妳跟我應該別再見面了。

貝蒂：那樣不是有點**太極端**了嗎？我還是可以過來看你啊。

路克：嗯，或許吧，我們可以試一陣子看看。

① **kiss** [kɪs] (v.) 親吻

例 Billy kisses his mom and dad goodnight before he goes to sleep.
比利睡覺前都會跟他爸媽親吻道晚安。

② **whisper** [`hwɪspɚ] (v.) 耳語；私語

例 Some teachers don't like it when students whisper to each other in class.
有些老師不喜歡學生上課時竊竊私語。

③ **gigantic** [dʒaɪ`gæntɪk] (adj.) 巨大的；龐大的

例 Outside their headquarters, the company placed a gigantic balloon with their logo on it.
這公司在他們的總部外面放了一個印有他們公司標誌的大汽球。

④ **liar** [`laɪɚ] (n.) 騙子

例 Everybody knows Jack is a big liar.
大家都知道傑克是個大騙子。

⑤ **imbecile** [`ɪmbəsl̩] (n.) 低能者；傻子

例 Even an imbecile could figure out this computer program.
就連智障都知道這個電腦程式怎麼用。

6 **move** [muv] (*v.*) 搬動；搬家

例 We've got so much stuff, it's going to take several days to move.

我們有太多的東西了，搬家要花好幾天的時間。

7 **rent** [rɛnt] (*v.*) 租

例 How long have you been renting this place?

這個地方你租多久了？

8 **apartment** [əˋpɑrtmənt] (*n.*) 公寓

例 I love the way you've decorated your apartment.

我喜歡你公寓的裝潢。

9 **original** [əˋrɪdʒənl] (*adj.*) 最初的；原本的

例 I know the idea isn't original.

我知道這個主意不是原創的。

10 **extreme** [ɪkˋstrim] (*adj.*) 極端的；偏激的

例 I also thought firing Michael for such a small mistake was extreme.

我也覺得為了這麼小的一個失誤就開除麥可是太極端了。

## 進階字彙

### 與戀愛有關的字

| | | |
|---|---|---|
| **affair** | [əˋfɛr] (*n.*) 婚外情；外遇 | |
| **betray** | [bɪˋtre] (*v.*) 背叛 | |
| **disloyal** | [dɪsˋlɔɪəl] (*adj.*) 不忠實的；不忠誠的 | |
| **secret** | [ˋsikrɪt] (*n.*) 秘密 | |
| **conceal** | [kənˋsil] (*v.*) 隱瞞 | |

### 居住的地方

| | | |
|---|---|---|
| **house** | [haʊs] (*n.*) 房子 | |
| **condominium** | [ˋkɑndəˏmɪnɪəm] (*n.*) 分戶出售的公寓 | |
| **penthouse** | [ˋpɛntˏhaʊs] (*n.*) 建築物頂層的豪華公寓 | |
| **suite** | [swit] (*n.*) 套房 | |
| **flat** | [flæt] (*n.*) 一層樓房 | |

文化總匯

美國人常常搬家，而搬家的原因若不是因為家長被公司調派到另一個地方去，就是因為在當地找不到工作，得到他處謀生，才必須搬家。家裡的小孩若還未滿十八歲，通常都會跟著父母搬遷，而十八歲以上的小孩就可以自己決定去留。

# ✏ Exercises 動手做

請從以下字彙中，挑出正確的單字填入空格內。

| whisper | gigantic | apartment | |
|---------|----------|-----------|------|
| liar | move | kiss | rent |

1. The piano is _____. Where are you going to put it?

2. Can you please help me _____ the TV to the other side of the room?

3. The baby's sleeping. Please _____ when you talk.

4. We want to _____ a house somewhere near the school

5. How many rooms does your _____ have?

1. 這台鋼琴好大，你要把它放在哪裡？
2. 能請你幫我把這台電視搬到房間的另一邊嗎？
3. 寶寶已經睡了，所以說話時請輕聲細語。
4. 我們想在學校附近租個房子。
5. 你的公寓有幾個房間？

解答 1. gigantic  2. move  3. whisper  4. rent  5. apartment

## Preview 字彙預習

| | |
|---|---|
| **behave** | 行為舉止；表現；守規矩 |
| **castle** | 城堡 |
| **chateau** | 城堡；法式別墅莊園 |
| **cruel** | 殘忍的；殘酷的 |
| **dining room** | 餐廳 |
| **enormous** | 巨大的；龐大的 |
| **fake** | 假的；偽裝的 |
| **friendly** | 親切的；友善的 |
| **inherit** | 繼承 |
| **kitchen** | 廚房 |
| **living room** | 起居室；客廳 |
| **manor** | 莊園 |
| **mansion** | 官邸；宅第；華廈美屋 |
| **neighborhood** | 附近；鄰居 |
| **palace** | 皇宮；宮殿 |
| **patio** | 天井；露台 |
| **remember** | 記得；想起 |
| **struggle** | 奮鬥；努力；掙扎 |
| **villa** | 別墅 |
| **yard** | 院子 |

平凡人心聲篇

*Kara and Jim are on their way home from visiting their friends, the Flagstaffs.*

Kara: I almost wish we hadn't paid them a visit. Their house is like a mansion.

Jim: And that new swimming pool – it's enormous.

Kara: I know. It's cruel world. Some people live like kings, while the rest of us struggle just to get by.

Jim: Before they inherited all that money, they were just normal people. Now, I don't know, they seem different.

Kara: Maybe they think we're not good enough for them any more.

翻譯

*卡拉跟吉姆剛拜訪完弗雷格斯塔夫一家人，正在回家的路上。*

卡拉：我真希望沒有來拜訪他們，他們的房子簡直像一棟豪宅。

吉姆：還有那個新的游泳池，好大喔。

卡拉：我知道，這真是個殘酷的世界，有些人過著國王般的生活，可我們其他人就要努力奮鬥才能活下去。

吉姆：在他們繼承那筆錢之前，他們也是普通人啊，現在呢，我不知道，他們看起來就是不一樣。

卡拉：也許他們覺得我們也不夠格可以當他們的朋友了呢。

*Willy and Laura Flagstaff are walking through their garden, just after Kara and Jim left.*

Willy: It was good to see them again. So few of our old friends stop by to visit us anymore.

Laura: Talking with them made me remember the good old days. We used to have so much fun before we moved here.

Willy: And our old neighborhood was much more friendly than this area. The way people behave here is so fake.

Laura: Jim and Kara don't know how lucky they are.

Willy: I was just thinking the same thing.

翻譯

*威利與蘿拉弗雷格斯塔夫在卡拉和吉姆離開後，走過家裡的花園。*

威利：能再看到他們真好，會來我們家玩的老朋友很少了。

蘿拉：跟他們說說話讓我**回想起**以前的好時光，在搬到這以前，我們一直有很多樂趣的。

威利：而且我們以前的**鄰居**也比這個區域的要**友善**多了，在這裡，人們的**行為表現**都好**做作**。

蘿拉：吉姆和卡拉不知道他們有多幸運呢。

威利：我的想法和你一樣。

①　**mansion** [ˋmænʃən] (*n.*) 官邸；宅第；華廈美屋

例 We took a tour of a beautiful mansion in Virginia.
我們在維吉尼亞州做了一趟豪宅之遊。

②　**enormous** [ɪˋnɔrməs] (*adj.*) 巨大的；龐大的

例 The house isn't very big, but the yard is enormous.
這房子雖然不大，不過院子超大的。

③　**cruel** [ˋkruəl] (*adj.*) 殘忍的；殘酷的

例 Today in class we read about this really cruel general.
今天的課堂上，我們讀到這位殘忍將軍的故事。

④　**struggle** [ˋstrʌgl] (*v.*) 奮鬥；努力；掙扎

例 After graduating from high school, Larry had to struggle
just to pay his bills on time.
自從高中畢業以後，賴瑞必須辛苦工作才有辦法準時付帳單。

⑤　**inherit** [ɪnˋhɛrɪt] (*v.*) 繼承

例 I inherited this boat from my uncle.
我從我舅舅那兒繼承了這艘船。

⑥ **remember** [rɪˋmɛmbə] (v.) 記得;想起

例 I can't remember the last time I laughed so hard.
我忘了上次笑得這麼開心是什麼時候的事了。

⑦ **neighborhood** [ˋnebəˌhud] (n.) 附近;鄰居

例 What I like most about this neighborhood is all the trees lining the streets.
這附近我最喜歡的就是街上成排的樹了。

⑧ **friendly** [ˋfrɛndlɪ] (adj.) 親切的;友善的

例 Mr. Elbert is friendly to everyone he meets.
艾伯特先生對他碰到的每個人都很友善。

⑨ **behave** [bɪˋhev] (v.) 行為舉止;表現;守規矩

例 Children in this private school are taught to behave properly.
這所私立學校的小孩都被教導得很循規蹈矩。

⑩ **fake** [fek] (adj.) 假的;偽裝的

例 Alice smiled when she saw me, but I could tell it was fake.
艾莉絲看到我時笑了,不過我可以看得出來那個笑容是假的。

## 🔖 進階字彙

### 豪華的住宅

| | |
|---|---|
| **villa** | [ˋvɪlə] (*n.*) 別墅 |
| **chateau** | [ʃæˋto] (*n.*) 城堡；法式別墅莊園 |
| **manor** | [ˋmænə] (*n.*) 莊園 |
| **castle** | [ˋkæsl] (*n.*) 城堡 |
| **palace** | [ˋpælɪs] (*n.*) 皇宮；宮殿 |

### 家裡的某個部分

| | |
|---|---|
| **living room** | [ˋlɪvɪŋ ˏrum] (*n.*) 起居室；客廳 |
| **kitchen** | [ˋkɪtʃɪn] (*n.*) 廚房 |
| **dining room** | [ˋdaɪnɪŋ ˏrum] (*n.*) 餐廳 |
| **patio** | [ˋpɑtɪ ˏo] (*n.*) 天井；露台 |
| **yard** | [jɑrd] (*n.*) 院子 |

文化總匯

在美國，一般人都會立遺囑，內容會交代哪個人可以拿多少錢，哪個人可以拿到什麼東西。通常人們在準備好遺囑後就會把它交給律師，並且不定期地修改內容。法律上也有規定，繼承多少金額的遺產就必須付一定比例的遺產稅。

# ✎ Exercises 動手做

請從以下字彙中，挑出正確的單字填入空格內。

| enormous | neighborhood | fake | |
|----------|--------------|------|------|
| mansion | behave | remember | cruel |

1. Do you _____ where we parked?

2. The _____ had nine bedrooms and five bathrooms.

3. Look at that _____ cow over there. It's as big as an elephant!

4. Are there any parks in the _____?

5. I knew the watch was _____. It was too cheap to be genuine.

1. 你記得我們把車停在哪兒嗎?
2. 豪宅裡有九間臥室及五間浴室。
3. 你看那邊那隻巨大的母牛,牠跟大象一樣大!
4. 這附近有什麼公園嗎?
5. 我知道這支錶是假的,它太便宜了所以不可能是真品。

解答 1. remember   2. mansion   3. enormous   4. neighborhood   5. fake

# Exercises 單字總復習 🔍 ✏️

**A** 選一最適合的字完成下列句子

1. I knew you lived in a big house, but I didn't realize it was as big as a _____!
   (A) mansion
   (B) photograph
   (C) gown
   (D) whisper

2. Don't get my cat angry, or she might _____ you.
   (A) struggle
   (B) borrow
   (C) trust
   (D) scratch

3. Bob was sad to learn the diamond ring he bought was _____.
   (A) serious
   (B) fake
   (C) brilliant
   (D) extreme

4. Drivers going down the _____ mountain road need to be very careful, or they might accidentally go over the cliff.
   (A) narrow
   (B) cruel
   (C) wealthy
   (D) friendly

5. We _____ rain, so you should bring your umbrella.
   (A) inherit
   (B) behave
   (C) anticipate
   (D) apologize

Many people are concerned that crime is rising and that their cities and ___(1)___ are becoming dangerous places to live. But are cities really more dangerous than they were 10 years ago, or do we just think they are?

Critics of the media point out how televised news reports focus on negative news and ___(2)___ cases, such as violent crime, ___(3)___ accidents, and scandals. We aren't shown much positive news, since it's less interesting and less entertaining. Hence, since many people watch the news every day, they come to feel the places they live in are unsafe. In reality, most cities are quite safe. ___(4)___, most of our neighbors are ___(5)___ people, and there are few murderers and criminals on the streets. The best way to start feeling safer may be to selectively choose where you get your news and how you interpret it.

1. (A) dates     (B) mansions     (C) neighborhoods     (D) gowns
2. (A) original     (B) extreme     (C) wealthy     (D) fake
3. (A) traffic     (B) rent     (C) liar     (D) imbecile
4. (A) Apologize     (B) Move     (C) Remember     (D) Inherit
5. (A) narrow     (B) friendly     (C) glamorous     (D) divorced

**A** 1. A  2. D  3. B  4. A  5. C

翻譯

1. 我知道你住在一棟大房子裡面，但是我不知道那跟大宅邸一樣大！
2. 不要惹我的貓生氣，不然牠會抓你。
3. 鮑伯很難過地發覺到他買的鑽石戒指是假的。
4. 走這條狹窄山路下山的駕駛要很小心，不然他們可能會不小心開出了懸崖。
5. 我們預料會下雨，所以你應該帶傘。

**B** 1. C  2. B  3. A  4. C  5. B

翻譯

許多人擔心犯罪增加，他們居住的城市和鄰近地區會變成危險的地方。但是城市真的比十年前危險的多嗎？或者這只是我們這麼想而已？

媒體評論家指出電視新聞如何集中在負面消息和極端的案例報導，例如暴力犯罪、交通事故以及醜聞。我們沒有被告知太多正面的新聞，因為那較不有趣也較不具娛樂性。 因此，由於許多人每天看新聞，他們開始覺得所居住的地方不安全。事實上，大多數的城市相當的安全。記住，我們大部分的鄰居都是友善的人，街上也很少會有殺人犯和罪犯。要開始感覺安全的最好方法或許是慎選你的新聞管道以及你解讀新聞的方式。

# 該學哪些字彙呢？

## ☑ 2000 個高頻字彙

每個英語學習者所必須知道的就是兩千個最常用的字。為什麼是最常用就最重要呢？原因在於我們日常生活中所說及聽到的字彙中，這兩千字就佔了百分之九十一，而當我們在閱讀時，也約莫有百分之八十五的字彙是從這兩千字中所出。事實上，調查顯示光是前一百個字就佔了整體的百分之四十九。

但其實你可能已經知道大部分常用的字，例如像 go，eat 等動詞，還有一些常見的形容詞像是 big，fast 等等。對這些高頻字彙所做的研究，已進行了有半個世紀多。字彙專家像保羅 • 耐森 (Paul Nation) 多年來就一直強調高頻字彙的重要，而大家也似乎終於開始注意這件事了。若想要對高頻字彙有更多的了解，你可以查閱 Collins Cobuild 進階英文字典，字典中在每個字之後，都有標明使用頻率

## ☑ 情境式與功能性字彙

除了這兩千個高頻字彙外，你需要學習的就是不同情境的用字範疇，比如工作時與休閒時的用字。而這正是本書所能給予你的，本書共有六個章節，目的是教你們認識常用字的使用方法，以及該如何應用到不同情境，其中包含了各種人際關係、工作、休閒旅遊等各種情境。

### A 情境用字：

例如，我們來看看單元 19：Leaving a company 的對話。
（對話中的目標字彙用粗體表示。）

*Two employees are talking in the employee lounge.*

Trisha: Are you all right, Bianca?

Bianca: I don't know. I've been working here for so many years. It's not **challenging** anymore.

Trisha: You sound **dissatisfied**. Are you thinking about quitting?

Bianca: I want to, but I'm afraid I won't find a new job.

Trisha: You can look for a job in your **spare time**. Then, **resign** here after you find a job you like.

*兩個同事在員工休息室聊天。*

翠莎　：你還好嗎，碧安卡？

碧安卡：我不知道，我已經在這裡工作好多年，這個工作再也沒什麼**挑戰**可言了。

翠莎　：你聽起來**不是很滿意**，你想辭職嗎？

碧安卡：我想啊，不過我怕找不到新工作。

翠莎　：你可以在**有空的時候**找工作啊，找到你喜歡的工作後，再把這裡的工作**辭掉**。

沒錯，這個情境大家應該都蠻熟悉的。特別留意目標字彙在情境中的關鍵性。碧安卡主要的問題是工作沒有挑戰性 (challenging)。翠莎則明確地指出碧安卡並不是很滿意 (dissatisfied) 現在的工作。然後建議碧安卡利用空閒時間 (spare time) 來找新工作。最後，她認為碧安卡應該先找到工作後再辭職 (resign)。

有注意到目標字彙是如何在對話中發揮重要性了嗎？若將這四個主要字挑出，整個對話就會顯的空洞。這就是本書運用的主要技巧，那就是教你立即將剛學的字彙應用在現實生活中。如果僅是將這些字列成一個長串，像在字典中的排列組合，那將無法幫助你理解它在現實生活中的用法，也無法感受到它溝通訊息的力量。

### 🅱 功能性用字
你也需要學習更多字來幫助你增強不同的語言功能，像是打招呼和道別的方式。讓我們來看以下對話。

*A woman wants to send a package to Australia.*

Woman: How much will this cost to send?

Worker: By **surface** mail or **airmail**?

Woman: Airmail.

Worker: Let me **weigh** it ... It will cost $17.00. And, you need to fill out this **customs declaration form**. Do you want to **insure** it?

Woman: No, that won't be **necessary**.

*有位女士想要寄個包裹到澳洲去。*

女士　　：寄這個要多少錢？

工作人員：要寄**水陸郵件**或是**航空郵件**？

女士　　：航空郵件。

工作人員：我來幫它**秤重**一下……要十七塊錢，還有，你必須填好這個**海關申報單**，這個包裹要**投保**嗎？

女士　　：不了，沒這個**需要**。

這是語言常見的功能，全世界的人都會用的。特別注意如何使用目標字彙發問及回答的技巧。郵局員工問女士是否需要投保她的包裹，而她回答說 No, that won't be necessary.（不了，沒這個需要）。我們在這裡看見了常見的表達方式，有可能發生在商店、郵局、或是一些服務業的場所。用這種方式學習字彙是很重要的，因為你可以理解何種句型會使用的何種字彙，也可知道該怎麼回應。

本書介紹的大量字彙貫穿了各種情境與功能。如果你能研讀全部，就能應付許多不同場合中的對話。這些字都是隨手可用，必能幫助你增進與英語人士對話的流暢度。

## ☑ 術語與專有名詞

當學會了許多不同的情境與功能用字，如本書所教的字彙，你就需要專注在與你日常生活中有關聯的字彙，這會因人而異，讓我用我自己生活中的真實故事作例子。

當我開始教授托福課程時，我知道自己必須了解如何用中文來解釋英文的文法結構。藉由一些同事的協助，我學到了文法專有名詞的中文譯名，比如像 "present perfect"「現在完成式」、"past conditional"「過去假設法」、"subject complement"「主詞補語」等等，經過了幾個禮拜的使用，我變得很會用中文來解釋英文文法。當然，大部分的人對這類字彙都不感興趣，所以他們也不會想學，不過以上就是一個很好的例子，說明了生活環境如何影響我們選擇語言學習的方式。

你大概會對某項特殊興趣或專業領域的英文用字有較深的涉獵，也

許是你熟悉的商業場合，也許你是眼鏡製造商，更或者你的興趣是攝影，這範圍可說是廣無邊際的。事實上，大部分的人對很多領域的術語均有所研究，如果你覺得自己對本身相關領域的字彙所知不多，我會建議你多讀些產業雜誌、報紙、或是網路上的文章。如此一來，你不只會學到與自己領域相關的字，同時也能學會許多在你專業上常用的動詞、形容詞和片語。

本書的每個單元都額外增加了十個與主題相關的單字，這些都是較為專門的用字，你可以多花些時間在所感興趣的主題上。以 Which job should I take?「我該接受那個工作呢？」這單元為例，內容跟選擇新工作有關，所以單元最後所額外增加的字如下：

- **full-time** 全職
- **part-time** 兼職
- **internship** 實習
- **partnership** 合夥
- **contractor** 立約人
- **insurance** 保險
- **holiday bonus** 假日津貼
- **retirement plan** 退休計劃
- **company car** 公司車
- **stock options** 股票訂金

這些都是跟工作型態以及公司福利有關的用字，所以當你在撰寫或談論這個主題時，他們對你會有很大的幫助。

# Chapter 3
# 商務活動、人力開發

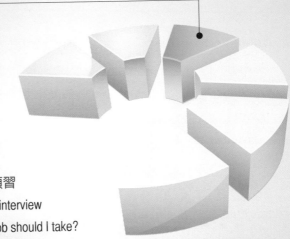

英語學習專欄 ❸

需要學多少字彙？

## Preview 字彙預習

| | |
|---|---|
| agent | 代理人 |
| commission | 佣金 |
| competitive | 競爭的 |
| computer literate | 會用電腦的 |
| filing | 檔案管理 |
| financial advisor | 財務顧問 |
| fluent | 流利的 |
| guarantee | 保證 |
| initiative | 主動進取 |
| investment broker | 投資仲介 |
| language skills | 語言能力 |
| personable | 容易相處的 |
| prior | 先前的 |
| qualified | 勝任的；具備必要條件的 |
| resume | 履歷 |
| salary | 薪資 |
| sales person | 業務員 |
| shorthand | 速記 |
| stock broker | 股票經紀人 |
| type | 打字 |

新鮮人面試篇

*Danny is interviewing for his first job.*

Ms. Mitchell: I see from your resume you don't have any prior experience. Do you feel you're qualified for the job?

Danny: Yes, ma'am. I have many skills that I can bring to your company.

Ms. Mitchell: Such as?

Danny: I can type 75 words per minute. I'm good with computers. And I'm fluent in Spanish.

Ms. Mitchell: This is a competitive field, so it's going to be hard for you at first. But I think you deserve a chance.

翻譯

*丹尼正在接受第一個工作的面試。*

米契爾小姐：我從你的**履歷**得知你**之前**沒有任何的工作經驗，你覺得你**資格符合**這個工作嗎？

丹尼　　：是的，女士。我有許多專長是貴公司需要的。

米契爾小姐：像是什麼？

丹尼　　：我每分鐘可**打**七十五個字，我精通電腦，我還能說**流利的**西班牙文。

米契爾小姐：這是個**競爭的**領域，剛開始對你來說可能有些困難，不過，我覺得可以給你一個機會。

**換工作篇**

*Theo Daniels, an experienced salesperson, is being interviewed for a job.*

Mr. Fremont: Why did you leave your last job?

Theo: I wasn't happy with the commissions they were paying.

Mr. Fremont: If we meet your salary demands, are you sure you can repeat the kind of success you've had elsewhere?

Theo: Mr. Fremont, I can guarantee it.

Mr. Fremont: I like your initiative. You've got the job.

**翻譯**

*提歐‧丹尼爾斯，一位經驗豐富的銷售人員，正在接受工作面試。*

弗瑞蒙先生：你為什麼要離開上一個工作？

提歐　　　：我不是很滿意他們所給的**佣金**。

弗瑞蒙先生：如果我們能滿足你對**薪水**的要求，你確定你能表現的跟之前一樣好嗎？

提歐　　　：弗瑞蒙先生，我**保證**我可以。

弗瑞蒙先生：我喜歡你的**主動積極**，你被錄取了。

① **resume** [͵rɛzju`me] (*n.*) 履歷

例 Experts say a resume shouldn't be more than one or two pages long.

專家說履歷的長度最好不要多於一或兩頁。

---

② **prior** [`praɪə] (*adj.*) 先前的

例 Tell me about any prior jobs you've had.

告訴我你先前做過的工作。

---

③ **qualified** [`kwɑlə͵faɪd] (*adj.*) 勝任的；具備必要條件的

例 In my opinion, the third candidate is the most qualified.

就我看來，第三個候選人最具備必要條件。

---

④ **type** [taɪp] (*v.*) 打字

例 Sherman is taking a class to learn how to type.

雪曼在修一門學習打字的課。

---

⑤ **fluent** [`fluənt] (*adj.*) 流利的

例 Sylvia, whose mother is from Italy, speaks fluent Italian.

席維雅會說流利的義大利文，因為她媽媽是義大利人。

6 **competitive** [kəm`pɛtətɪv] (*adj.*) 競爭的

例 In competitive fields, people often work overtime and rarely take vacations.

競爭激烈的領域裡，人們常常要加班，而且很少渡假。

7 **commission** [kə`mɪʃən] (*n.*) 佣金

例 Some sales people rely on commission for all of their income.

有些業務員的收入全都要倚賴佣金。

8 **salary** [`sælərɪ] (*n.*) 薪資

例 Besides a base salary, the job paid a monthly bonus based on each person's performance.

除了底薪外，這工作還依每個人的表現給予每月紅利。

9 **guarantee** [ˌgærən`ti] (*v.*) 保證

例 It's easy to guarantee something, but it's much harder to actually do it.

要保證會做某事很容易，不過要真正做到就難得多。

10 **initiative** [ɪ`nɪʃɪˌetɪv] (*n.*) 主動進取

例 Workers were encouraged to show personal initiative on the job.

員工們都被鼓勵在工作上要表現個人的主動進取。

## 🔖 進階字彙

| | | |
|---|---|---|
| **computer literate** | [kəm`pjutə `lɪtərɪt] (adj.) | 會用電腦的 |
| **language skills** | [`læŋgwɪdʒ `skɪlz] (n.) | 語言能力 |
| **shorthand** | [`ʃɔrt͵hænd] (n.) | 速記 |
| **filing** | [`faɪlɪŋ] (n.) | 檔案管理 |
| **personable** | [`pɜsn̩əb!] (adj.) | 容易相處的 |

有佣金的工作

| | | |
|---|---|---|
| **sales person** | [`selz͵pɜsn̩] (n.) | 業務員 |
| **stock broker** | [`stɑk `brokə] (n.) | 股票經紀人 |
| **investment broker** | [ɪn`vɛstmənt `brokə] (n.) | 投資仲介 |
| **financial advisor** | [faɪ`nænʃəl əd`vaɪzə] (n.) | 財務顧問 |
| **agent** | [`edʒənt] (n.) | 代理人 |

文化總匯

在美國應徵工作，履歷表裡的內容通常包括：應
徵者對這個工作的抱負與展望、教育背景、歷年
的工作經驗及工作上的成就、在那些工作做了幾
年、專長技能等等；履歷內並不列年齡、生日、
自傳，而且整份履歷最好是一到兩頁的長度。

# ✏ Exercises 動手做

請從以下字彙中，挑出正確的單字填入空格內。

| commission | guarantee | competitive | |
|---|---|---|---|
| type | initiative | resume | qualified |

1. This company is so _____, only the best employees last long.

2. How many words can you _____ per minute?

3. The lazy worker was criticized for not showing any _____.

4. Do you receive a _____ for every TV you sell?

5. In America, people do not write down their birth date on their _____.

1. 這家公司非常的競爭，只有最好的員工才能做得久。
2. 你每分鐘可以打幾個字？
3. 那個懶惰的員工被批評為沒有表現出主動進取。
4. 你每賣一部電視機都會得到佣金嗎？
5. 在美國，人們都不會在履歷上註明他們的生日。

解答 1. competitive  2. type  3. initiative  4. commission  5. resume

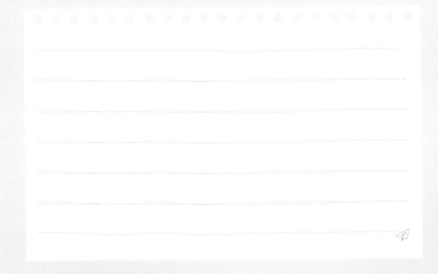

## Preview 字彙預習

| | |
|---|---|
| **accept** | 接受；答應；同意 |
| **accommodate** | 通融；提供方便 |
| **benefit** | 福利 |
| **company car** | 公司車 |
| **contractor** | 承包商 |
| **full-time** | 專職的；全職的 |
| **generous** | 慷慨的；大方的 |
| **holiday bonus** | 額外假期 |
| **imply** | 暗示；意味著 |
| **insurance** | 保險 |
| **internship** | 實習 |
| **negative** | 負面的；否定的；消極的 |
| **overtime** | 加班 |
| **paid vacation** | 有薪假期 |
| **partnership** | 合夥關係；合資公司 |
| **part-time** | 兼職的 |
| **position** | 職位 |
| **positive** | 正面的；肯定的；積極的 |
| **retirement plan** | 退休計劃 |
| **stock options** | 認股權 |

選擇工作篇

*Colleen applied to work at several companies. She got two job offers.*

Colleen: I don't know which job I should take.

Trenton: Start by asking yourself what's positive and negative about each one.

Colleen: OK. The job at Allied Computers pays well. But I'm not totally happy with the benefits.

Trenton: What about the job at Solar Industries?

Colleen: It also pays well. However, they implied there will be some overtime. I don't want that.

翻譯

*可琳應徵了幾家公司，她得到其中兩家公司的工作機會。*

可琳：我不知道該接受哪個工作。

崔頓：從問你自己每個工作的**正負面**開始吧。

可琳：好吧。聯合電腦的薪水不錯，不過我不是很滿意他們的**福利**。

崔頓：那太陽系工業的工作呢？

可琳：他們給的薪水也不錯，但他們**暗示**了偶爾得**加班**，而我不想要那樣。

**爭取福利篇**

*Colleen calls Allied Computers about their job offer.*

Ms. Westwood: Have you decided to accept the position?

Colleen: Well, your offer is very generous, but I have one small request.

Ms. Westwood: What is it?

Colleen: Instead of seven days paid vacation, could you make it 10?

Ms. Westwood: Yes, I think we can accommodate you there.

**翻譯**

*可琳打電話給聯合電腦要談談他們所提供的工作機會。*

西木女士：你已經決定要**接受**這個**職位**了嗎？

可琳　　：嗯，你們薪水給得很**慷慨**，不過我有個小小的要求。

西木女士：是什麼呢？

可琳　　：可以要求把七天的**有薪假期**改成十天嗎？

西木女士：可以啊，我想我們可以**通融**你的需求。

# 核心字彙

MP3 22

①**positive** [ˋpɑzətɪv] (*adj.*) 正面的；肯定的；積極的

例 One positive thing about my job is it's near my house.
我的工作有個好處就是它離我家很近。

②**negative** [ˋnɛgətɪv] (*adj.*) 負面的；否定的；消極的

例 A couple of our colleagues think Wendy has a negative attitude.
我們有些同事覺得溫蒂的態度很消極。

③**benefit** [ˋbɛnəfɪt] (*n.*) 福利

例 Could you tell me about the job benefits?
你能告訴我這工作的福利如何嗎？

④**imply** [ɪmˋplaɪ] (*v.*) 暗示；意味著

例 At the meeting, Christine implied she was going to quit.
在會議中，克莉絲汀暗示她要辭職。

⑤**overtime** [ˋovəˌtaɪm] (*n.*) 加班

例 If I have to work overtime again, I'll go crazy!
如果我還得再加班的話，我會發瘋！

112

6. **accept** [ək`sɛpt] (v.) 接受；答應；同意

   例 Before Friday, they need to know if I'll accept the offer.
   在星期五以前，他們就要知道我是否接受他們提供的條件。

7. **position** [pə`zɪʃən] (n.) 職位

   例 Mike is happy with his position in the company.
   麥克對他在公司裡的職位很滿意。

8. **generous** [`dʒɛnərəs] (adj.) 慷慨的；大方的

   例 It's a generous amount, but I still have to refuse.
   那額度給的很大方，不過我仍然得拒絕。

9. **paid vacation** [`ped ve`keʃən] (n.) 有薪假期

   例 All the employees in our firm get paid vacation every year.
   我們公司裡的所有員工每年都有有薪假期。

10. **accommodate** [`əkɑmə‚det] (v.) 通融；提供方便

    例 I hope you can accommodate these changes to the schedule.
    我希望你能通融一下時程表裡的這些變更。

## 進階字彙

### 工作型態

| | | |
|---|---|---|
| **full-time** | [ˋfulˋtaɪm] (*adj.*) | 專職的；全職的 |
| **part-time** | [ˋpɑrtˋtaɪm] (*adj.*) | 兼職的 |
| **internship** | [ˋɪntɜnˏʃɪp] (*n.*) | 實習 |
| **partnership** | [ˋpɑrtnəˏʃɪp] (*n.*) | 合夥關係；合資公司 |
| **contractor** | [ˋkɑntræktə] (*n.*) | 承包商 |

### 職工福利

| | | |
|---|---|---|
| **insurance** | [ɪnˋʃʊrəns] (*n.*) | 保險 |
| **holiday bonus** | [ˋhɑləˏde ˋbonəs] (*n.*) | 額外假期 |
| **retirement plan** | [rɪˋtaɪrmənt ˋplen] (*n.*) | 退休計劃 |
| **company car** | [ˋkʌmpənɪ ˋkɑr] (*n.*) | 公司車 |
| **stock options** | [ˋstɑk ˋɑpʃənz] (*n.*) | 認股權 |

文化總匯

在美國，兼職跟全職工作的福利大不相同，兼職工作無法拿到的福利包括了保險、假日領薪、公司配車、公司配用筆記型電腦……等等。領月薪的人，就算超時工作，也沒有加班費，只有領時薪的人才有加班費可拿，加班費的計算方式如下：前八個小時是依時薪計算，第九到十二小時是依時薪一點五倍計算，第十三到十六小時則是兩倍。

# ✎ Exercises 動手做

請從以下字彙中，挑出正確的單字填入空格內。

| accommodate | benefit | paid vacation | |
|---|---|---|---|
| imply | positive | overtime | accept |

1. Everyone likes Bill because of his _____ attitude.

2. The small company could not _____ all its employees' requests.

3. Do you mean to _____ something with that comment?

4. Of course I'll _____ the promotion!

5. I get a _____ every year, but I can never decide where I should travel to.

1. 大家喜歡比爾，因為他有正面積極的態度。
2. 那間小公司沒辦法照顧到所有員工的需求。
3. 你想用那個聲明暗示什麼嗎？
4. 我當然會接受這晉升的機會！
5. 我每年都有段有薪休假，不過都無法決定要去哪裡玩。

解答　1. positive　2. accommodate　3. imply　4. accept　5. paid vacation

## Preview 字彙預習

| | |
|---|---|
| **agree** | 同意 |
| **compromise** | 妥協；和解 |
| **conduct** | 引導；實施；進行 |
| **contract** | 合約；契約 |
| **copyright** | 版權；著作權 |
| **deal** | 生意；交易 |
| **distribution** | 配貨；舖貨；物流 |
| **estimate** | 估計；判斷 |
| **exclusive** | 專用的；獨家的 |
| **handle** | 處理 |
| **import** | 進口；輸入 |
| **license** | 執照；給某人或某事執照 |
| **market analysis** | 市場分析 |
| **marketing** | 行銷；市場行銷學 |
| **negotiate** | 談判；協商 |
| **profitable** | 有利潤的 |
| **propose** | 提議；計劃 |
| **sales volume** | 銷售量 |
| **term** | 任期；條件；術語；期限 |
| **unit** | 單位 |

提案篇

*Representatives from two companies are discussing a business deal.*

Mr. Simons: You're saying you'd like to import our whole line of products?

Mr. Wang: Exactly. We think they would sell very well in our local market.

Mr. Simons: And you'll handle all the marketing and distribution?

Mr. Wang: Yes, we will.

Mr. Simons: It's an interesting idea. Now let's talk about the details.

翻譯

*兩位公司的代表正在討論生意。*

席門斯先生：你是說你想要**進口**我們產品線的所有產品嗎？

王先生　　：完全正確，我們覺得這些產品可以在我國市場銷售得很好。

席門斯先生：那麼，你們會**處理**所有的**行銷**與**舖貨**嗎？

王先生　　：是的，我們會。

席門斯先生：蠻有趣的主意，我們現在就來談點細節問題吧。

細節篇

*Mr. Wang and Mr. Simons discuss the details of the deal.*

Mr. Simons: What kind of sales volume do you expect?

Mr. Wang: We estimate sales of 100,000 units per year.

Mr. Simons: Really? And, what is that estimate based on?

Mr. Wang: We conducted a full market analysis. Here are the results.

Mr. Simons: I must say I like what I see so far. This deal may be very profitable for both of our companies.

翻譯

王先生和席門斯先生商討生意細節。

席門斯先生：你們預期有多少的銷售量？

王先生　　：我們估計每年會有十萬個單位。

席門斯先生：是嗎？那麼，預估量是根據什麼而得的？

王先生　　：我們進行了全盤的市場分析，結果就得到了這個數字。

席門斯先生：我得說到目前為止我都很滿意，這筆生意可能會為我們雙方帶來非常豐厚的利潤。

① **import** [ɪm`port] (v.) 進口；輸入

例 Are there any other companies importing that type of product?

有別的公司在進口那類產品嗎？

② **handle** [`hændl] (v.) 處理

例 Our agent in Tokyo is handling our affairs there.

我們在東京的代理商會幫我們處理那邊的事務。

③ **marketing** [`markɪtɪŋ] (n.) 行銷；市場行銷學

例 Do you know who's in charge of marketing here?

你知道是誰掌管這裡的行銷事務嗎？

④ **distribution** [ˌdɪstrə`bjuʃən] (n.) 配貨；舖貨；物流

例 There have been a few problems with our distribution system.

我們的配貨物流系統有一些問題。

⑤ **sales volume** [`selz `valjəm] (n.) 銷售量

例 This year's sales volume should be better than ever.

今年的銷售量應該會比往年好。

⑥ **estimate** [ˋɛstəˌmet] (v.) 估計；判斷

> 例 It's hard to estimate how much shipping charges will be.
> 很難估計運費要花多少錢。

⑦ **unit** [ˋjunɪt] (n.) 單位

> 例 Once we receive the 1,000 units, we'll send the rest of the payment.
> 一旦我們收到一千個單位，我們就會付尾款。

⑧ **conduct** [kənˋdʌkt] (v.) 引導；實施；進行

> 例 The food company conducted a survey to see how people liked their canned vegetables.
> 為了要了解人們是否喜歡他們公司生產的罐頭蔬菜，這個食品公司進行了一項問卷調查。

⑨ **market analysis** [ˋmɑrkɪt əˋnæləsɪs] (n.) 市場分析

> 例 Maybe we should hire an outside company to help us with the market analysis.
> 也許我們該請外面的公司來幫我們做市場分析。

⑩ **profitable** [ˋprɔfɪtəbl̩] (adj.) 有利潤的

> 例 Since the board of directors did not feel the project would be profitable, they cancelled it.
> 因為董事會的成員不覺得這個計劃會帶來利潤，所以他們將它取消了。

## 合約常用字

| | | |
|---|---|---|
| **contract** | [ˋkɑntrækt] (n.) | 合約；契約 |
| **license** | [ˋlaɪsn̩s] (n./v.) | 執照／給某人或某事執照 |
| **copyright** | [ˋkɑpɪˏraɪt] (n.) | 版權；著作權 |
| **exclusive** | [ɪkˋsklusɪv] (adj.) | 專用的；獨家的 |
| **term** | [tɜm] (n.) | 任期；條件；術語；期限 |

## 談判常用字

| | | |
|---|---|---|
| **deal** | [dil] (n./v.) | 生意／交易 |
| **negotiate** | [nɪˋgoʃɪˏet] (v.) | 談判；協商 |
| **compromise** | [ˋkɑmprəˏmaɪz] (n./v.) | 妥協；和解 |
| **propose** | [prəˋpoz] (v.) | 提議；計劃 |
| **agree** | [əˋgri] (v.) | 同意 |

文化總匯

大部分的美國公司都有自己的市場分析小組，公司會先用問卷或電話調查消費者的喜好，再依據調查結果進行分析預測，以提出迎合消費大眾的新產品的研發案。新產品上市前，會先生產試用品，請大眾試用，並依其反應改善產品，最後才推出正式商品到市場上販賣。

# ✎ Exercises 動手做

請從以下字彙中，挑出正確的單字填入空格內。

| sales volume | profitable | conduct | |
|---|---|---|---|
| handle | import | units | estimate |

1. The _____ for the "Titan" line of products should reach 500,000 units this year.

2. How easy is it to _____ products in that country?

3. From now on, Mr. Jones will _____ sales and marketing for Southeast Asia.

4. How many _____ would you like to order?

5. If we market these items well, total sales could be very _____ for us.

1. 「泰坦」線的商品今年的銷售量會到達五十萬個。

2. 進口產品到那個國家容易嗎？

3. 從現在起，瓊斯先生會處理東南亞地區的銷售與行銷。

4. 你想訂購多少單位呢？

5. 如果這些商品能行銷得當，整體的銷售將會帶來非常可觀的利益。

解答 1. sales volume　2. import　3. handle　4. units　5. profitable

## Preview 字彙預習

| | |
|---|---|
| agriculture | 農業（展） |
| arrange | 安排 |
| brochure | 小冊子 |
| client | 客戶 |
| collectibles | 收藏（展） |
| conference | 協議會 |
| deliver | 投遞；運送 |
| display | 陳列展示 |
| electronics | 電子（展） |
| exhibition | 展覽 |
| exposition | 博覽會 |
| furniture | 傢俱（展） |
| international | 國際的 |
| outstanding | 顯著的；傑出的 |
| overseas | 海外的；國外的 |
| sample | 樣本；樣品 |
| show | 秀展 |
| specifications | 規格 |
| supplier | 供應商 |
| trade | 貿易（展） |

## 供應商篇

*At a large booth, a man talks to a salesperson.*

Man: What are the specifications of this motherboard?

Salesperson: Here's a brochure with all the details.

Man: Thanks. Tell me, do you have a lot of overseas clients?

Salesperson: As a matter of fact, 40 percent of our clients are from outside of Taiwan.

Man: That's good. We're looking for a new supplier, and we want someone with international experience.

## 翻譯

*有個男人在跟某大攤位的業務員談話。*

男士 ：這塊主機板的**規格**是什麼？

銷售員：這本**小冊子**裡有所有的詳細資料。

男士 ：謝謝。告訴我，你們有很多**外國客戶**嗎？

銷售員：事實上，我們百分之四十的客戶都來自台灣以外的地區。

男士 ：那很好，我們正在找新的**供應商**，而且我們想找有**國際**經驗的公司。

**樣品篇**

*At another booth, a woman looks at a display of batteries.*

Woman: Do you have any samples I can take?

Salesperson: Not here we don't, but we can arrange to send you some.

Woman: I'll only be here a few days.

Salesperson: That's plenty of time. I can call my office. They'll deliver the samples to your hotel.

Woman: Outstanding. I'll write down my hotel name and room number. Oh, and here's my name card.

**翻譯**

*在另一個攤位，有位女士正在看電池的展示。*

女士　：你們有任何**樣品**可以拿嗎？

銷售員：這裡沒有，不過我們可以**安排**送一些給您。

女士　：我只會在這裡停留幾天喔。

銷售員：那還蠻久的，我可以打個電話給我們公司，他們會把樣品**送到**您的飯店。

女士　：**太好了**，我會留下我的飯店名稱和房間號碼。喔，還有，這是我的名片。

① **specifications** [ˌspɛsəfəˈkeʃənz] (*n.*) 規格

例 Are you sure these specifications are correct?

你確定所有規格都正確嗎？

---

② **brochure** [broˈʃʊr] (*n.*) 小冊子

例 We handed out 5,000 brochures at the show.

我們在展覽時發出了五千份的小冊子。

---

③ **overseas** [ˈovɚˈsiz] (*adj.*) 海外的；國外的

例 Using the Internet, it's easy to perform overseas banking transactions.

透過網際網路，海外的銀行業務就會很容易執行。

---

④ **client** [ˈklaɪənt] (*n.*) 客戶

例 Several clients have complained about our after-sales service.

有幾個客戶抱怨過我們的售後服務。

---

⑤ **supplier** [səˈplaɪɚ] (*n.*) 供應商

例 Since our main supplier went bankrupt, we'll have to find a new one.

因為我們主要的供應商破產了，所以我們必須要找個新的。

---

⑥ **international** [ˌɪntɚˋnæʃənḷ] (*adj.*) 國際的

例 With companies from more than 20 countries attending, the show will have a real international flavor.
有來自二十多個國家的公司參與，這個展覽將會真正具有國際性。

⑦ **sample** [ˋsæmpḷ] (*n.*) 樣本；樣品

例 Mr. McKinley was impressed with the samples we sent him.
麥金里先生對我們送給他的樣品印象深刻。

⑧ **arrange** [əˋrendʒ] (*v.*) 安排

例 Before you arrive, I'll arrange a hotel for you to stay at.
在你到達前，我會安排好你要住的飯店。

⑨ **deliver** [dɪˋlɪvɚ] (*v.*) 投遞；運送

例 This shipment must be delivered within two weeks.
這個貨物得在兩個星期內送達。

⑩ **outstanding** [ˋaʊtˋstændɪŋ] (*adj.*) 顯著的；傑出的

例 Your speech at the conference was outstanding.
你在會議中的演講真是太傑出了。

## 進階字彙

### 不同型式的展示會

**conference** [ˋkɑnfərəns] (*n.*) 協議會

**exhibition** [ˋɛksəˋbɪʃən] (*n.*) 展覽

**display** [dɪˋsple] (*n./v.*) 陳列展示

**exposition** (expo) [͵ɛkspəˋzɪʃən] (*n.*) 博覽會

**show** [ʃo] (*n.*) 秀展

### 一般型態的展覽

**electronics** [ɪ͵lɛkˋtrɑnɪks] (*n.*) 電子（展）

**trade** [tred] (*n.*) 貿易（展）

**agriculture** [ˋægrɪ͵kʌltʃə] (*n.*) 農業（展）

**collectibles** [kəˋlɛktəb!z] (*n.*) 收藏（展）

**furniture** [ˋfɜnɪtʃə] (*n.*) 傢俱（展）

文化總匯

全美最大的電腦展 COMDEX，一年一度會在拉斯維加斯舉行，全球電腦相關產業的廠商都會前來共襄盛舉，展出他們最新研發的科技產品，很多大公司的老闆或總裁會應邀發表演講。

# ✎ Exercises 動手做

請從以下字彙中，挑出正確的單字填入空格內。

| deliver | outstanding | international | |
|---------|-------------|--------------|--------|
| brochure | arrange | samples | client |

1. This year, we'll make a full-color _____ to show off our products.

2. When I travel to Germany, I'll bring several _____ to give our clients.

3. The man at the furniture store said he'll _____ the sofa today.

4. This display is _____. It should attract a lot of business.

5. Ms. Lee will _____ to meet with us while we're in Hong Kong.

1. 今年我們會製作全彩的小冊子來秀出商品。
2. 我到德國出差時,會帶幾個樣品給我們的客戶。
3. 傢俱店的人說他今天會把沙發送來。
4. 這個展示會很傑出,應該可以招攬很多生意。
5. 當我們到了香港,李小姐會安排跟我們見面。

解答 1. brochure  2. samples  3. deliver  4. outstanding  5. arrange

## Preview 字彙預習

| appetizer | 開胃菜；開胃小吃 |
|---|---|
| cash | 現金 |
| check | 支票 |
| coupon | 兌換券；優待券 |
| credit card | 信用卡 |
| delicious | 美味的；好吃的 |
| dessert | 點心；餐後甜點 |
| favorite | 最喜歡的 |
| guest | 客人 |
| hors d'ouevres | （法式）開胃小菜 |
| insist | 堅持 |
| main course | 主菜 |
| menu | 菜單 |
| recommend | 推薦；介紹 |
| side order | 主菜以外附帶叫的菜 |
| suggest | 建議；提議 |
| terrific | 非常好的；很棒的 |
| variety | 多樣化；種類 |
| voucher | 證件；收據 |
| waiter | 男服務生 |

## Andrew's 精選對話

 MP3 27

**點餐篇**

*A manager of a plastics company takes an important foreign client to dinner.*

Client: This is a nice place. Do you come here often?

Manager: Yes, it's one of my favorite restaurants.

Client: The menu is so long. Is there anything you'd recommend?

Manager: I suggest we order one of the set meals. That way you can try a variety of dishes.

Client: Good idea. That will make ordering easier, since the menu is all in Chinese!

**翻譯**

*一家塑膠公司的經理帶了一位重要的外國客戶去吃晚餐。*

客戶：這個地方不錯，你常來嗎？

經理：是啊，它是我**最喜歡**的餐廳之一。

客戶：**菜單**好長喔，你要**推薦**什麼菜色嗎？

經理：我**建議**我們可以點個套餐，這樣你就可以試試**不同**的菜色。

客戶：好主意，那會讓點餐容易些，因為這個菜單上都是中文！

## 結帳篇

*It's time to pay the bill.*

Client:     The meal was delicious.

Manager:  I'm glad you liked it. Waiter, check please.

Client:     Here, I'll get it.

Manager:  No, you're my guest. I insist on paying.

Client:     Thank you. If you ever make it to New York, there are some terrific restaurants I'd like to take you to.

## 翻譯

*付帳時間到了。*

客戶：這一頓飯**真好吃**。

經理：很高興你喜歡。**服務生**，請買單。

客戶：來，我來付。

經理：不行，你是我的**客人**，我**堅持**要請客。

客戶：謝謝，如果你有**機會**到紐約來，我很願意帶你到幾間**很棒的**餐廳去。

① **favorite** [ˋfevərɪt] (*adj.*) 最喜歡的

例 Sour and spicy soup is my favorite.

我最喜歡酸辣湯了。

② **menu** [ˋmɛnju] (*n.*) 菜單

例 These pictures on the menu make it easier to order.

菜單上的這些照片使點菜變得容易些。

③ **recommend** [ˌrɛkəˋmɛnd] (*v.*) 推薦；介紹

例 Let's ask the waitress to recommend something.

我們請服務小姐推薦些東西。

④ **suggest** [səˋdʒɛst] (*v.*) 建議；提議

例 I suggest we sit somewhere near the garden.

我建議我們坐在靠近花園的地方。

⑤ **variety** [vəˋraɪətɪ] (*n.*) 多樣化；種類

例 I've never seen such a great variety of desserts!

我沒見過這麼多種的點心！

⑥ **delicious** [dɪ`lɪʃəs] (*adj.*) 美味的；好吃的

例 It wasn't the most delicious meal I've ever had, but it wasn't bad.

這不是我吃過最好吃的一餐，不過也算不錯了。

⑦ **waiter** [`wetɚ] (*n.*) 男服務生

例 The next time the waiter walks by, tell him we're ready to order.

下次服務生經過時，告訴他我們準備點餐了。

⑧ **guest** [gɛst] (*n.*) 客人

例 You're the guest, so you can order first.

你是客人，所以你可以先點菜。

⑨ **insist** [ɪn`sɪst] (*v.*) 堅持

例 I insist on taking you out for lunch.

我堅持要帶你出去吃午餐。

⑩ **terrific** [tə`rɪfɪk] (*adj.*) 非常好的；很棒的

例 The band is terrific, wouldn't you say?

這個樂團很棒，你不覺得嗎？

## 🖈 進階字彙

**上菜的內容**

| | | |
|---|---|---|
| **appetizer** | [ˋæpəˌtaɪzə] (*n.*) | 開胃菜；開胃小吃 |
| **hors d'ouevres** | [ɔrˋdɜvz] (*n.*) | （法式）開胃小菜 |
| **main course** | [men kors] (*n.*) | 主菜 |
| **dessert** | [dɪˋzɜt] (*n.*) | 點心；餐後甜點 |
| **side order** | [saɪd ˋɔrdə] (*n.*) | 主菜以外附帶叫的菜 |

**付款方式**

| | | |
|---|---|---|
| **cash** | [kæʃ] (*n.*) | 現金 |
| **check** | [tʃɛk] (*n.*) | 支票 |
| **credit card** | [ˋkrɛdɪt ˋkard] (*n.*) | 信用卡 |
| **coupon** | [ˋkupɑn] (*n.*) | 兌換券；優待券 |
| **voucher** | [ˋvautʃə] (*n.*) | 證件；收據 |

**文化總匯**

在美國，朋友一起出去吃飯的話，帳單是每個人均分，或各付各的；若是商業餐敘，通常由公司付帳，這筆款項有含稅，在每年公司報稅時，可以退稅；若是男女朋友一起用餐，則通常是由男方付帳。

# ✏ Exercises 動手做

請從以下字彙中，挑出正確的單字填入空格內。

| suggest | recommend | delicious | |
|---------|-----------|-----------|---------|
| favorite | gust | waiter | variety |

1. Their salad bar has a good _____ of vegetables to choose from.

2. The food was so _____, I'm going to tell all my friends to come here.

3. I'll tell the _____ to bring us more napkins.

4. What's your _____ kind of food?

5. Since they're out of Greek salad today, I'd _____ the chef's salad instead.

1. 他們的沙拉吧有很多樣的蔬菜可供選擇。
2. 這裡的食物好好吃，我要叫所有的朋友都來吃。
3. 我會告訴服務生給我們多幾條餐巾。
4. 你最喜歡的食物是什麼？
5. 因為他們今天的希臘沙拉賣完了，所以我推薦主廚沙拉。

解答 1. variety   2. delicious   3. waiter   4. favorite   5. recommend

# Exercises 單字總復習 🔍 ✏

**A** 選一最適合的字完成下列句子

1. Several _____ at the hotel complained about the loud noise from the nearby construction site.
   (A) brochures        (B) specifications
   (C) guests          (D) resumes

2. Because of her _____ school records, Gina was admitted to a famous university.
   (A) negative       (B) profitable
   (C) fluent           (D) outstanding

3. health insurance and paid vacations are just two of the many _____ we offer our emplyees.
   (A) benefits       (B) clients
   (C) samples       (D) positions

4. The division was closed because it was not _____.
   (A) prior            (B) fluent
   (C) delicious       (D) profitable

5. We _____ that within 6 months, we will control 30% of the market.
   (A) conduct       (B) estimate
   (C) import         (D) type

**B** 將下列空格填入最適合的單字

Micro technology is one of the most important elements of modern electronic products. Everything from cell phones to computers is getting smaller and smaller. At the same time, consumers are ___(1)___ on more and more features in their personal electronic products. Fortunately, advances in battery technology and power designs allow us to use our ___(2)___ machines longer than ever.

As these products become more sophisticated, profits from leading electronics companies continue to be very high. That's because advances in production methods have allowed them to create larger volumes of goods, with better and better ___(3)___, at lower and lower prices. Of course, companies spend billions of dollars on research to help them stay in the lead and remain ___(4)___. As the micro technology revolution unfolds, one trend is clear: Year after year, electronics companies will have to give us a ___(5)___ of new products, for less money, and in smaller and smaller packages.

1. (A) implying      (B) insisting  (C) recommending (D) guaranteeing
2. (A) favorite      (B) negative (C) sample      (D) qualified
3. (A) specifications (B) positions (C) commissions (D) waiters
4. (A) prior         (B) delicious (C) competitive (D) international
5. (A) salary        (B) unit      (C) market analysis (D) variety

**A** 1. C　2. D　3. A　4. D　5. B

翻譯

1. 旅館的好幾個客人抱怨從附近工地傳來的巨大噪音。
2. 因為她優異的學業記錄，吉娜得到這所知名大學的入學許可。
3. 健康保險和有薪休假只是我們提供給員工的眾多福利中的兩項而已。
4. 這個部門已經關閉了，因為它不賺錢。
5. 我們估計在六個月中，我們將會控制百分之三十的市場。

**B** 1. B　2. A　3. A　4. C　5. D

翻譯

微電腦科技是現代電子產品最重要的元素之一。從手機到電腦，每樣東西都越來越小。同時，消費者強調個人電子產品要有越來越多的特色。幸好，電池科技和電力設計的進步讓我們使用特別喜愛機器的時間可以比以往久。

由於這些產品日趨精密，電子公司的龍頭的獲利也維持在非常高的水平。那是因為生產技術的進步讓他們可以更大量地製造出規格越來越好、價格越來越低廉的產品。當然，公司花費數十億元於研究上，幫助他們維持領先的地位以及保持競爭性。當微電腦科技革命一展開，潮流的趨勢就很明顯了：每年電子公司都必須給我們多種更便宜、體積越來越小的新產品。

# 需要學多少字彙呢？

這是我常被問到的有趣問題，而關於這個議題也引起相當大的爭論。有些人會專注於英語母語人士口說中的平均用字。其他人則選擇五千或一萬個字，並給予自己不同的理由來學習這麼多的字。

我已經提過二千個高頻字彙的重要性，這二千字中有大部分在國中與高中就學過了。除了這些字，增加額外的二千到三千字絕對會給你足夠的用字來應付一般的會話，並了解你所讀到與聽到的絕大部分。不過，請記住以下的要點：

## ☑ 多花一點時間 確實「認識」一個字

首先，要知道何謂認識一個字。常常發生一種情形就是，學習者通常都急於學習大量的字，他們會去買字彙量很多的書，然後嘗試這些字彙全都背下來。

如我們所知，這種學習方式通常只會讓單字的記憶停留一到兩天。之後，就會忘掉大部分，想要真正認識一個字，需要花更多的時間。

研究員約翰‧利得建議，要認得一個字，就必須知道它的意義、拼法、發音、文法型態、使用頻率、搭配方法、使用限制，以及詞彙的接收理解與運用產出的知識。這並不表示你需要花好幾個小時去讀一個字。不過，這意味著當你在學一個生字時，你不應只學習表面上的拼法與意義。本書提供了字彙所屬的上下文、詞性、發音及

中文翻譯等，這些都可以更確實地認識字彙應有的條件。

## ☑ 片語亦不可或缺

有太多人都只專注於學習單一或不常用的字，而往往忽略了片語，這是很危險的，因為片語佔了我們日常生活字彙的大部分。這就是《多角建構英文片語》的創作之因，《多角建構英文片語》為本書系之另一章，而就像這本字彙書一樣，也是運用上下文的技巧來教片語。

# Chapter 4
# 辦公室、人事問題

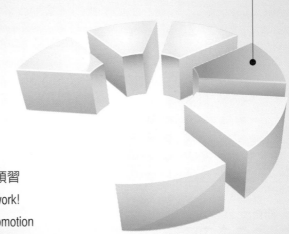

- **Preview** 字彙預習
- **Day 15** Great work!
- **Day 16** The promotion
- **Day 17** A new manager
- **Day 18** Getting fired
- **Day 19** Leaving a company
- **Exercises** 單字總複習

英語學習專欄 ④
「閱讀」是增加字彙的最佳途徑

## Preview 字彙預習

| | |
|---|---|
| **admire** | 欣賞；欽佩 |
| **bonus** | 紅利；獎金；額外津貼 |
| **compare** | 比較；對照 |
| **competitor** | 競爭者；對手 |
| **complain** | 抱怨；發牢騷；控訴 |
| **correspondence** | 通信聯繫 |
| **crucial** | 決定性的；重要的 |
| **dislike** | 討厭 |
| **envy** | 忌妒；羨慕 |
| **important** | 重要的 |
| **inconsequential** | 不重要的 |
| **insignificant** | 微不足道的 |
| **invaluable** | 無價的 |
| **meaningless** | 無意義的 |
| **motivate** | 驅動；激發 |
| **realize** | 領悟；了解到 |
| **respect** | 敬重；尊敬；敬佩 |
| **support** | 支持；擁護 |
| **tolerate** | 容忍；不干預 |
| **underestimate** | 低估 |

老闆稱讚篇

*Natalie is praised by her boss for a job well done.*

Boss: I just received a fax from our client in Brazil. They're placing a $50,000 order with us.

Natalie: Excellent. After they compared prices between us and our competitors, they finally realized our prices are the lowest.

Boss: That's part of it, but you deserve a lot of the credit too.

Natalie: Thanks. I did send quite a few e-mails to them this month.

Boss: Good correspondence is invaluable to every company. Don't underestimate its importance.

翻譯

*娜塔莉因為工作做得很好而受到老闆的誇讚。*

老　闆：我剛收到巴西客戶發來的傳真，他們跟我們下了張金額五萬元的訂單。

娜塔莉：太棒了，在**比較**了我們跟其他**競爭者**的價格後，他們終於**了解**我們是最低價的。

老　闆：那只是一部分，妳的功勞也很大。

娜塔莉：謝啦，這個月我確實寄了不少電子郵件給他們。

老　闆：對每家公司來說，良好的**通信聯繫**是**無價的**，別**低估**了它的重要性。

加薪篇

*Jacky's paycheck is larger than usual.*

Jacky: I'm not complaining or anything, but my paycheck is for $200 too much.

Boss: That's a bonus. You did a great job last month.

Jacky: I did?

Boss: Sure. You may not know it, but your colleagues all respect you. They see you working hard, and it motivates them to do better.

Jacky: Oh. Well, my dad always said doing a good job is more important than getting a good salary. Of course, a big paycheck is nice, too.

翻譯

*傑克的薪水比往常的還多。*

傑克：我不是要發牢騷或什麼的，只是我的薪水多了兩百塊錢。

老闆：那是紅利，你上個月做得很好。

傑克：我有嗎？

老闆：當然有，你可能不知道，不過你的同事都很敬佩你，他們看到你努力地工作，那驅使他們想做得更好。

傑克：喔，我爸總是說把工作做好比薪水好更重要。當然啦，能得到高薪也是滿好的。

① **compare** [kəm`pɛr] (*v.*) 比較；對照

例 I'd like to compare these offers before making a decision.
在決定前我想多比較一下這些報價。

---

② **competitor** [kəm`pɛtətə] (*n.*) 競爭者；對手

例 If we don't treat our customers well, they'll take their business to one of our competitors.
如果我們不善待我們的客戶，他們會把生意交給我們的對手。

---

③ **realize** [`riə͵laɪz] (*v.*) 領悟；了解到

例 The letter said they realized they made a mistake and will take steps to correct it.
信上說他們了解他們造成的錯誤，且願意逐步修正它。

---

④ **correspondence** [͵kɔrə`spɑndəns] (*n.*) 通信聯繫

例 Make sure to save a copy of all your correspondence with your clients.
要確定留存一份你跟所有客戶通信資料的備份。

---

⑤ **invaluable** [ɪn`væljəbḷ] (*adj.*) 無價的

例 The help I received from my more experienced colleagues was invaluable.
我從經驗較豐富的同事那兒所獲得的幫助是無價的。

---

⑥ **underestimate** [ˌʌndɚˋɛstəˌmet] (*v.*) 低估

例 Never underestimate even the smallest competitor.
即使是力量微弱的對手，永遠別低估他的實力。

⑦ **complain** [kəmˋplen] (*v.*) 抱怨；發牢騷；控訴

例 Mr. O'Conners called to complain about the damaged shipment.
歐康納先生打電話來投訴貨物損毀的事。

⑧ **bonus** [ˋbonəs] (*n.*) 紅利；獎金；額外津貼

例 As the company's profits were very high last year, each employee received a bonus.
這公司去年的盈餘很高，每個員工都獲得了額外的獎金。

⑨ **respect** [rɪˋspɛkt] (*v.*) 敬重；尊敬；敬佩

例 People respect Miss Lanterns for being a fair and patient boss.
人們會尊敬連坦絲小姐是因為她是個公平又有耐心的老闆。

⑩ **motivate** [ˋmotəˌvet] (*v.*) 驅動；激發

例 The supervisor gave a speech to motivate the factory workers.
這個上司說了些話來激發工廠員工。

## 🔖 進階字彙

**描述事情**

| | |
|---|---|
| **important** | [ɪmˋpɔrtn̩t] (*adj.*) 重要的 |
| **crucial** | [ˋkruʃəl] (*adj.*) 決定性的；重要的 |
| **meaningless** | [ˋminɪŋlɪs] (*adj.*) 無意義的 |
| **insignificant** | [ˌɪnsɪgˋnɪfəkənt] (*adj.*) 微不足道的 |
| **inconsequential** | [ɪnˌkɑnsəˋkwɛnʃəl] (*adj.*) 不重要的 |

**對同事的感覺**

| | |
|---|---|
| **admire** | [ədˋmaɪr] (*v.*) 欣賞；欽佩 |
| **support** | [səˋport] (*v.*) 支持；擁護 |
| **envy** | [ˋɛnvɪ] (*v.*) 忌妒；羨慕 |
| **dislike** | [dɪsˋlaɪk] (*v.*) 討厭 |
| **tolerate** | [ˋtɑləˌret] (*v.*) 容忍；不干預 |

文化總匯

以前美國公司的對外聯絡及溝通的工具都會使用電話與傳真，如今因為網際網路的發達，電子郵件已經取代了電話或傳真，因為跨州甚至跨國的電話與傳真費用沒有電子郵件便宜，所以用電子郵件可以節省公司在通訊上的龐大支出。

# ✎ Exercises 動手做

請從以下字彙中，挑出正確的單字填入空格內。

| correspondence | realize | underestimate | |
|---|---|---|---|
| bonus | invaluable | motivate | compare |

1. Do you _____ how much trouble you've caused?

2. With this year's Christmas _____, I'm going to buy a new TV.

3. The coach tried his best to _____ the losing team.

4. The general told the soldiers not to _____ their enemy.

5. This electronic dictionary has been _____. It has saved me so much tim.

翻譯

1. 你知道你惹了多少麻煩嗎？
2. 有了今年的耶誕獎金，我要買台新電視。
3. 這個教練想盡辦法來激發這支輸了比賽的隊伍。
4. 將軍告訴士兵們別低估他們的敵人。
5. 這個電子辭典是無價的，它幫我省下太多時間了。

解答 1. realize 2. bonus 3. motivate 4. underestimate 5. invaluable

## Preview 字彙預習

| | |
|---|---|
| **buddy** | 好夥伴;好搭檔;好朋友 |
| **CEO** | 執行長 |
| **confident** | 有信心的 |
| **demote** | 降職 |
| **deserve** | 應受;該得 |
| **disappointed** | 失望的 |
| **employee** | 雇員;員工 |
| **experience** | 經驗;閱歷 |
| **fire** | 解僱 |
| **hire** | 僱用 |
| **know-how** | 實際知識;技能;竅門 |
| **lay off** | 裁員 |
| **manager** | 經理 |
| **political** | 政治化的;行政的 |
| **president** | 總裁;總經理 |
| **promote** | 晉升;升遷 |
| **promotion** | 升遷;晉級 |
| **relax** | 放輕鬆 |
| **supervisor** | 主任;課長 |
| **vice-president** | 副總裁;副總經理 |

# Andrew's 精選對話

## 升遷宣佈前篇

*Today Mr. Reed will announce which employee got promoted.*

Laurie: Oh no, there's Mr. Reed. He's talking to Scott.

Roselyn: He can't give the promotion to Scott. You deserve it.

Laurie: Do I? This company is so political. It's not about what you know, but who you know.

Roselyn: But you've got so much experience. Relax, you'll get it.

Laurie: I wish I were as confident as you are.

## 翻譯

*今天，里得先生會宣佈哪個雇員可以得到升遷。*

羅莉　：喔不，里得先生在那裡，他在跟史考特說話。

若莎琳：他不能把這個**升遷**機會給史考特，妳才是**應該得到**它的人。

羅莉　：是嗎？這個公司很**政治化的**，那跟你知道什麼沒關係，而跟你認識什麼人有關係。

若莎琳：不過妳**經驗豐富**啊，**放輕鬆點**，妳一定可以升遷的。

羅莉　：我真希望我跟妳一樣**有信心**。

## 升遷結果揭曉篇

*Mr. Reed is speaking to Scott about the promotion.*

Scott: So, do you have good news for me?

Mr. Reed: Scott, you're a good employee. And your dad and I have been buddies for a long time.

Scott: Thank you, I …

Mr. Reed: But I need someone with more know-how for this job. I'm going to give it to Laurie. I hope you're not disappointed.

Scott: No, of course not. Maybe next time.

## 翻譯

*里得先生正跟史考特談有關升遷的事。*

史考特　：那麼，你有什麼好消息要告訴我嗎？

里得先生：史考特，你是個很好的**員工**，而且你老爸跟我一直都是**好夥伴**。

史考特　：謝謝，我……

里得先生：不過，我需要個更**知道技術層面**的人來擔任這個職務，我會把這個升遷機會給羅莉，我希望你不要**失望**。

史考特　：當然不會，也許下次還有機會。

①　**promotion** [prə`moʃən] (*n.*) 升遷；晉級

　　例 How much more will you earn if you get the promotion?
　　如果你得到晉升，可以多賺多少錢？

②　**deserve** [dɪ`zɝv] (*v.*) 應受；該得

　　例 Few colleagues thought Martin deserved to be the project manager.
　　沒幾個同事認為馬丁應該當專案經理。

③　**political** [pə`lɪtɪkḷ] (*adj.*) 政治化的；行政的

　　例 Everyone knew Donald was fired for political reasons.
　　大家都知道唐諾是因為一些政治上的原因而被解僱的。

④　**experience** [ɪk`spɪrɪəns] (*n.*) 經驗；閱歷

　　例 How much experience do you have working with computers?
　　你用電腦工作的經驗有多少？

⑤　**relax** [rɪ`læks] (*v.*) 放輕鬆

　　例 Relax, it's Friday afternoon. The weekend's almost here!
　　放輕鬆，現在是禮拜五下午，週末就快到了！

⑥ **confident** [ˋkɑnfədənt] (*adj.*) 有信心的

例 If you're not confident of the case, I'll handle it for you.
如果你沒信心做這個案子，我會幫你處理。

⑦ **employee** [ˏɪmpləˋi] (*n.*) 雇員；員工

例 The small trading company only had six employees.
那個小貿易公司只有六個員工。

⑧ **buddy** [ˋbʌdɪ] (*n.*) 好夥伴；好搭檔；好朋友

例 Harrison and Philip quickly became good buddies at work.
哈里森和菲力普很快就在工作上成為好搭檔。

⑨ **know-how** [ˋnoˏhaʊ] (*n.*) 實際知識；技能；竅門

例 Fixing cars takes mechanical know-how.
修理車子需要有機械的實際知識。

⑩ **disappointed** [ˏdɪsəˋpɔɪntɪd] (*adj.*) 失望的

例 If you're disappointed about that performance review,
you should talk to your supervisor about it.
如果你對那個複審的結果感到失望，你應該跟你的上司談談。

## 📌 進階字彙

### 公司職位

| | | |
|---|---|---|
| **supervisor** | [ˌsupəˋvaɪzə] (n.) | 主任；課長 |
| **manager** | [ˋmænɪdʒə] (n.) | 經理 |
| **vice-president** | [ˋvaɪs ˋprɛzədənt] (n.) | 副總裁；副總經理 |
| **president** | [ˋprɛzədənt] (n.) | 總裁；總經理 |
| **CEO** (chief executive officer) | [ˋsi ˋɪ ˋo] (n.) | 執行長 |

### 人事政策

| | | |
|---|---|---|
| **hire** | [haɪr] (v.) | 僱用 |
| **fire** | [faɪr] (v.) | 解僱 |
| **lay off** | [ˋle ˌɔf] (v.) | 裁員 |
| **promote** | [prəˋmot] (v.) | 晉升；升遷 |
| **demote** | [dɪˋmot] (v.) | 降職 |

美國的職場生態裡，員工的年齡並不重要，所以升遷的機會並不會受年齡影響。會影響升遷的大致有兩個主要原因，一是工作能力，另一是人事背景。要看公司的人事決策者是受什麼因素的影響大些，來決定員工的升遷。

# ✏ Exercises 動手做

請從以下字彙中，挑出正確的單字填入空格內。

| buddy | relax | political | |
|---|---|---|---|
| employee | confident | experience | disappointed |

1. We need to hire another _____ to help us run the shop.

2. I'd like you to meet Chris, a good _____ of mine.

3. Working in our Tokyo branch was a very good _____ for me.

4. I hope you're not _____ about having to work overtime.

5. Remember to be _____ when you introduce our products to clients.

翻譯

1. 我們還需僱用另一個員工來幫我們管理這家店。
2. 我來跟你介紹克里斯，我的一位好夥伴。
3. 在東京分行工作過，對我而言是個非常好的經驗。
4. 我希望你對必須加班的事不會感到沮喪。
5. 當你在介紹我們的產品給客戶時，記得要有信心。

解答 1. employee 2. buddy 3. experience
4. disappointed 5. confident

## Preview 字彙預習

| | |
|---|---|
| **competition** | 競爭 |
| **executive** | 主管 |
| **experienced** | 經驗豐富的 |
| **fair** | 公正的 |
| **introduce** | 介紹 |
| **knowledgeable** | 博學的；有見識的 |
| **obey** | 遵守；聽從 |
| **offer** | 給予；提供 |
| **order** | 命令 |
| **refreshing** | 使人耳目一新的 |
| **rely** | 依賴；仰仗；指望 |
| **replace** | 取代；替換 |
| **rewarding** | 有收穫的；有報酬的 |
| **stressful** | 緊張的；壓力重的 |
| **strict** | 嚴謹的；要求嚴格的 |
| **superior** | 上司 |
| **tiresome** | 累人的；使人疲勞的 |
| **transfer** | 轉調；調動 |
| **unpredictable** | 出乎預料的 |
| **unreasonable** | 不合理的；過分的 |

# Andrew's 精選對話

## 初次見面篇

*Tim Thorton is the new manager at the Paris branch of his company.*

Tim: Allow me to introduce myself. I'm Tim Thorton. I just transferred here from New York.

Bob: Glad to know you, Tim. I'm Bob Jayward. Are you replacing Larry as the branch manager?

Tim: Yes, I am. By the way, why did Larry leave, if I might ask.

Bob: I heard he was offered an executive position at some Wall Street firm.

Tim: That's funny. I just came here from New York. It looks like we traded countries.

## 翻譯

*提姆‧梭頓是他的公司派來巴黎分公司的新經理。*

提姆：讓我自我介紹一下，我是提姆‧梭頓，我剛從紐約**調**到這裡來。

鮑伯：很高興認識你，提姆。我是鮑伯‧傑沃。你是**取代**賴瑞在分公司的經理職務嗎？

提姆：是的。還有，如果可以的話，我想順便問一下，賴瑞為什麼要離職。

鮑伯：我聽說華爾街的某公司要**提供**他一個**主管級**的職務。

提姆：那可真有趣，我才從紐約來。看來我們好像是交換國家了。

新官上任篇

*Leona has just been promoted to manager.*

Tiffany: You're my superior now. Does that mean I have to obey your orders?

Leona: It's not like that. We're still part of the same team. And we're still friends, right?

Tiffany: Of course we are. I was just giving you a hard time.

Leona: Tiff, I need you on my side. You know how much competition there is around here. I'm relying on your support.

Tiffany: Don't worry, girlfriend. I'm here for you.

翻譯

*里歐娜才剛升為經理。*

蒂芬妮：妳現在是我的**頂頭上司**囉，那是不是表示我都要**聽從**妳的**命令**？

里歐娜：不是那樣的，我們還是在同個團隊裡啊，而且，我們依然還是朋友，對吧？

蒂芬妮：我們當然是啦，我只是想讓妳覺得不好過。

里歐娜：蒂芬，我需要妳在我的左右，妳知道這裡有多麼的**競爭**，我真的要**仰仗**妳的支持。

蒂芬妮：別擔心，好朋友，我會在這裡支持妳的。

---

① **introduce** [ˌɪntrəˋdjus] (v.) 介紹

　　例 You'll have to introduce me to Stephen some time.
　　找個時間妳一定得把我介紹給史蒂芬認識。

---

② **transfer** [trænsˋfɝ] (v.) 轉調；調動

　　例 I told my boss I don't want to transfer overseas.
　　我告訴我老闆我不想調到國外。

---

③ **replace** [rɪˋples] (v.) 取代；替換

　　例 I understand why you're quitting, but it's going to be hard
　　to replace you.
　　我了解你為何要辭職，不過要找人頂替你將會很難。

---

④ **offer** [ˋɔfɚ] (v.) 給予；提供

　　例 Can I offer you a cup of coffee while you're waiting?
　　在您等待時，我可以給您一杯咖啡嗎？

---

⑤ **executive** [ɪgˋzɛkjutɪv] (n.) 主管、執行者

　　例 The executives met in the conference room to discuss the
　　quarterly report.
　　主管們在會議室裡開會討論季報告。

---

⑥ **superior** [səˋpɪrɪə] *(n.)* 上司

例 In our company, we address everybody, including our superiors, by their first name.

在我們公司裡，我們都用名字來互稱對方，包括稱呼我們的上司。

⑦ **obey** [oˋbe] *(v.)* 遵守；聽從

例 Don't you hate obeying people who are less qualified than you are?

你不覺得要聽命於條件比你還差的人很討厭嗎？

⑧ **order** [ˋɔrdə] *(n.)* 命令

例 The way she said it, it sounded more like an order than a request.

她說那件事的樣子比較像個命令而不像請求。

⑨ **competition** [ˏkɑmpəˋtɪʃən] *(n.)* 競爭

例 Competition for good jobs has always been strong in this area.

在這個領域要找個好工作，一向是非常競爭。

⑩ **rely** [rɪˋlaɪ] *(v.)* 依賴；仰仗；指望

例 I rely on my assistant to get a lot of things done.

我仰仗我助理的幫忙來完成很多工作。

## 🖈 進階字彙

### 敘述調職的狀況

| | | |
|---|---|---|
| **rewarding** | [rɪˋwɔrdɪŋ] *(adj.)* | 有收穫的；有報酬的 |
| **refreshing** | [rɪˋfrɛʃɪŋ] *(adj.)* | 使人耳目一新的 |
| **stressful** | [ˋstrɛsful] *(adj.)* | 緊張的；壓力重的 |
| **tiresome** | [ˋtaɪrsəm] *(adj.)* | 累人的；使人疲勞的 |
| **unpredictable** | [ˌʌnprɪˋdɪktəbl̩] *(adj.)* | 出乎預料的 |

### 描述主管的方式

| | | |
|---|---|---|
| **experienced** | [ɪkˋspɪrɪənst] *(adj.)* | 經驗豐富的 |
| **knowledgeable** | [ˋnɑlɪdʒəbl̩] *(adj.)* | 博學的；有見識的 |
| **fair** | [fɛr] *(adj.)* | 公正的 |
| **strict** | [strɪkt] *(adj.)* | 嚴謹的；要求嚴格的 |
| **unreasonable** | [ʌnˋriznəbl̩] *(adj.)* | 不合理的；過分的 |

文化總匯

在美國的公司裡，職位高的人，如行銷經理，或是技術性高的人，如高級工程師，只要在該領域有出色的表現，很容易就成為其他公司高薪挖角的對象，因為在人力市場裡這類的人才供不應求，所以在美國常常都有這種被挖角而跳槽的事發生。

# ✏ Exercises 動手做

請從以下字彙中，挑出正確的單字填入空格內。

| executive | competition | transfer | |
| rely | order | introduce | obey |

1. Employees who don't ＿＿＿＿＿＿ Mr. Chadway are quickly fired.

2. I ＿＿＿＿＿＿ on my computer so much, I couldn't get anything done without it.

3. At the end of this week, I'll ＿＿＿＿＿＿ to another department.

4. Now that the economy has improved, ＿＿＿＿＿＿ isn't as bad as it used to be.

5. When are you going to ＿＿＿＿＿＿ me to your boyfriend?

1. 不服從查威先生的員工很快就會被開除了。
2. 我非常依賴我的電腦，少了它我就無法完成任何事。
3. 這個禮拜末，我會轉調到另一個部門。
4. 既然經濟已有改善，競爭就沒像以前那麼激烈了。
5. 你什麼時候才要介紹我給你男朋友認識？

解答　1. obey　2. rely　3. transfer　4. competition　5. introduce

# Getting Fired

遭到開除

## Preview 字彙預習

| | |
|---|---|
| **appreciate** | 感激；體會 |
| **blunt** | 直率的；直言不諱的 |
| **customer** | 顧客 |
| **dedicated** | 投入的；專注的 |
| **disastrous** | 悲慘的 |
| **dishonest** | 不誠實的；不正直的 |
| **effort** | 努力 |
| **embezzle** | 盜用；侵占 |
| **hesitate** | 躊躇；猶豫；說話吞吞吐吐 |
| **incompetent** | 不能勝任的 |
| **inefficient** | 沒效率的 |
| **lazy** | 怠惰的 |
| **lie** | 說謊 |
| **private** | 私下的；個人的；非公開的 |
| **sabotage** | 破壞；從事破壞活動 |
| **selfish** | 自私的；只顧自己的 |
| **spill** | 打翻；濺灑 |
| **spy** | 當間諜；暗中監視 |
| **steal** | 偷 |
| **work force** | 人力資源 |

**工作表現不佳篇**

*After working at a fast food restaurant for three months, Franklin loses his job.*

Manager: Franklin, I need to speak with you for a moment, in private.

Franklin: Yes, Mr. Sanders.

Manager: Sit down, son. I don't know any nice way to say this. We're going to have to let you go.

Franklin: Let me go? I don't understand. What did I do wrong?

Manager: We know you've made efforts to do a good job. But, well, look. You keep giving the customers the wrong order. You spill at least three drinks a day. And, you often show up late. I'm sorry, there's no other way.

**翻譯**

*在一個速食店工作三個月後，法蘭克林丟了他的飯碗。*

經理 ：法蘭克林，我得跟你私下談一談。

法蘭克林：好的，山德斯先生。

經理 ：坐一下吧，孩子，我不知道怎麼說比較好，我們必須請你走。

法蘭克林：要我走？我不明白，我做錯什麼了嗎？

經理 ：我們知道你很努力想把事情做好，不過，你一直給錯客人點的食物，一天最少打翻三次飲料，而且你常遲到，我很抱歉，不過沒有別的辦法了。

## 公司營運不佳篇

*Angela's company is having hard times. They're looking for ways to save money.*

Angela: You asked to see me, Ms. Williams?

Ms. Williams: Yes, I did. I'm short on time, so I have to be blunt. Our third quarter earnings were disastrous. We need to cut costs by 30 percent, so …

Angela: I think I know what's coming. I'm being laid off, aren't I?

Ms. Williams: Not just you — one third of our work force. You've been a dedicated member of our team. If there's anything I can do for you, don't hesitate to ask.

Angela: I appreciate that. Excuse me, I better go clean out my desk.

### 翻譯

*安琪拉的公司營運不佳，他們正在找省錢的方法。*

安琪拉　：妳要見我嗎，威廉斯小姐？

威廉斯小姐：是啊，我時間不多，所以我就**直說**了，我們第三季的收入慘**不忍睹**，因此我們必須削減百分之三十的開支，所以……

安琪拉　：我想我知道接下來妳要說什麼了，我會被裁員，是嗎？

威廉斯小姐：不只妳，公司三分之一的**人力**都會遭到裁撤，妳一直是我們團隊中很有**貢獻的**一員，如果有什麼我能幫忙的，請別**客氣**。

安琪拉　：很**感激**妳的提議，抱歉，我最好回去清桌子了。

① **private** [ˋpraɪvɪt] (*adj.*) 私下的；個人的；非公開的

例 We should discuss this in a private place, not at the office.
我們應該在比較隱密的地方談這件事，而不是在辦公室裡談。

② **effort** [ˋɛfət] (*n.*) 努力

例 Everybody gave an extra effort to beat the deadline.
大家都格外盡力要在時限內完成。

③ **customer** [ˋkʌstəmə] (*n.*) 顧客

例 One of our customers has a question about the new exercise bicycles.
我們有個客戶對新的健身單車提了一個問題。

④ **spill** [spɪl] (*v.*) 打翻；潑灑

例 Be careful not to spill your coffee on my notebook computer.
小心別把你的咖啡潑灑在我的筆記型電腦上。

⑤ **blunt** [blʌnt] (*adj.*) 直率的；直言不諱的

例 Ernest's blunt way of speaking made his colleagues uncomfortable.
恩尼斯有話直說的方式讓他的同事很不自在。

⑥ **disastrous** [dɪz`æstrəs] *(adj.)* 悲慘的

例 Nobody could agree on anything. The meeting was disastrous.
沒有人同意任何事，這個會議真悲慘。

⑦ **work force** [`wɜk `fɔrs] *(n.)* 人力資源

例 We consider our work force to be the best in the industry.
我們認為這個產業裡我們有最好的人力資源。

⑧ **dedicated** [`dɛdə͵ketɪd] *(adj.)* 投入的；專注的

例 These days, it's rare to meet a totally dedicated employee at any company.
近來很難在任何公司看到完全盡心投入的員工了。

⑨ **hesitate** [`hɛzə͵tet] *(v.)* 躊躇；猶豫；說話吞吞吐吐

例 Bill hesitated when he was asked about how much money he earned.
被問到賺多少錢時，比爾顯得吞吞吐吐的。

⑩ **appreciate** [ə`priʃɪ͵et] *(v.)* 感激；體會

例 Although I appreciate your offer, I can't accept it.
雖然我很感激你提供的機會，不過我不能接受。

## 🖊 進階字彙

| | | |
|---|---|---|
| **lazy** | [`lezɪ] (*adj.*) 怠惰的 | |
| **incompetent** | [ɪn`kɑmpətənt] (*adj.*) 不能勝任的 | |
| **inefficient** | [ɪnə`fɪʃənt] (*adj.*) 沒效率的 | |
| **selfish** | [`sɛlfɪʃ] (*adj.*) 自私的；只顧自己的 | |
| **dishonest** | [dɪs`ɑnɪst] (*adj.*) 不誠實的；不正直的 | |

| | | |
|---|---|---|
| **lie** | [laɪ] (*v.*) 說謊 | |
| **steal** | [stil] (*v.*) 偷 | |
| **embezzle** | [ɪm`bɛzl] (*v.*) 盜用；侵占 | |
| **spy** | [spaɪ] (*v.*) 當間諜；暗中監視 | |
| **sabotage** | [`sæbə͵tɑʒ] (*v.*) 破壞；從事破壞活動 | |

美國人只要年滿十五歲就可以開始工作，因為缺乏工作經驗，所以也只能到一些不需要什麼經驗的地方工作，像是服飾店、百貨店、唱片行、書店……等，尤其速食店的店員絕大部分都是高中生；通常他們所領的薪資是政府所規定的最低工資 (minimum wage)。

# ✐ Exercises 動手做

請從以下字彙中，挑出正確的單字填入空格內。

| disastrous | dedicated | customer | |
|---|---|---|---|
| hesitate | blunt | effort | work force |

1. If I were you, I wouldn't _____ to accept the deal.

2. Fifty-four percent of our company's _____ is made up of women.

3. Mr. Chapman tends to speak very directly, so don't be surprised if he's _____ when he talks to you.

4. Our stock recently lost 23 percent of its value. What a _____ month!

5. As long as you make an _____ to do your job well, that's good enough.

翻譯

1. 如果我是你,我會毫不猶豫地接受這個生意。
2. 我們公司的人力有五成四是女性。
3. 查普曼先生向來是有話直說,所以如果他對你直言不諱的話,也別太驚訝。
4. 我們的股價最近跌了兩成三,這個月真悲慘啊!
5. 只要你有盡力在做事,那就夠好了。

解答　1. hesitate　2. work force　3. blunt　4. disastrous　5. effort

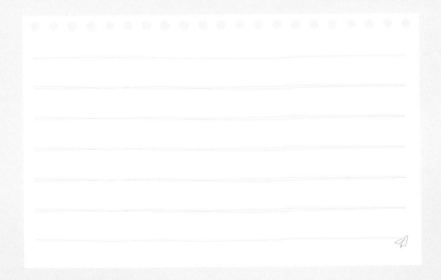

## Preview 字彙預習

| | |
|---|---|
| **boring** | 無聊的 |
| **challenging** | 有挑戰性的 |
| **difficult** | 艱難的 |
| **dissatisfied** | 不滿的 |
| **dull** | 單調乏味的；令人生厭的 |
| **early retirement** | 提早退休 |
| **elderly** | 年長的 |
| **fishing** | 釣魚 |
| **interesting** | 有趣的 |
| **nonsense** | 胡說；廢話 |
| **partner** | 夥伴；搭檔 |
| **pension** | 退休金；養老撫恤金 |
| **repetitive** | 反覆的 |
| **resign** | 辭職 |
| **retire** | 退休 |
| **severance package** | 遣散費 |
| **spare time** | 有空的時候；空閒時間 |
| **step down** | 退位；離職 |
| **strange** | 奇怪的；感覺陌生的 |
| **stuck** | 被困住的 |

**轉職篇**

*Two employees are talking in the employee lounge.*

Trisha: Are you alright, Bianca?

Bianca: I don't know. I've been working here for so many years. It's not challenging anymore.

Trisha: You sound dissatisfied. Are you thinking about quitting?

Bianca: I want to, but I'm afraid I won't find a new job.

Trisha: You can look for a job in your spare time. Then, resign here after you find a job you like.

**翻譯**

*兩個同事在員工休息室聊天。*

翠莎　：你還好嗎，碧安卡？

碧安卡：我不知道，我已經在這工作好多年，這個工作再也沒有什麼**挑戰性**了。

翠莎　：你聽起來**不是很滿意**，你想辭職嗎？

碧安卡：我想啊，不過我怕找不到新工作。

翠莎　：你可以在**空閒的時候**找工作啊，找到你喜歡的工作後，再把這裡的工作**辭掉**。

**退休篇**

*At age 67, Jacob is retiring from his job.*

Dwight: It's going to be strange without you here. I thought you'd never retire.

Jacob: Me too. We've been partners for, what, 35 years?

Dwight: At least. Maybe I should leave too.

Jacob: Nonsense. Leave when you're ready, not because of me.

Dwight: Still, while you're out there fishing and living the good life, I'll be stuck in here.

**翻譯**

*雅各就要在六十七歲時退休了。*

頓特：你不在這裡，這裡會變得很奇怪，我還以為你永遠不會**退休**的。

雅各：我本來也這樣想，我們成為**夥伴**已經，幾年，三十五年了嗎？

頓特：最少有吧，也許我也該離開了。

雅各：**胡說**，等你準備好時再離開，而不是因為我而離開。

頓特：不過，當你出外**釣魚**享受好生活時，我還**困**在這兒呢。

① **challenging** [ˋtʃælɪndʒɪŋ] (*adj.*) 有挑戰性的

　例 Her dream is to find a job that is challenging and high paying.

　她的夢想是找到一份高薪又有挑戰性的工作。

---

② **dissatisfied** [dɪsˋsætɪsˌfaɪd] (*adj.*) 不滿的

　例 Everyone gets dissatisfied with their job from time to time.

　每個人偶爾都會對他們的工作感到不滿。

---

③ **spare time** [ˋspɛr ˋtaɪm] (*n.*) 有空的時候；空閒時間

　例 Since he became division manager, Danny hasn't had any spare time.

　自從丹尼當了部門經理後，他就沒有什麼空閒時間了。

---

④ **resign** [rɪˋzaɪn] (*v.*) 辭職

　例 Think very carefully before you resign from your position.

　你要辭職前可要小心地考慮清楚。

---

⑤ **strange** [strendʒ] (*adj.*) 奇怪的；感覺陌生的

　例 What's that strange smell in my office?

　我辦公室裡的那個怪味道是什麼？

⑥ **retire** [rɪ`taɪr] (*v.*) 退休

例 I'll retire after I have a million dollars saved.

等存了一百萬元後我就會退休。

⑦ **partner** [`pɑrtnɚ] (*n.*) 夥伴；搭檔

例 Both the partners thought opening a branch office in Mexico was a good idea.

這兩個合夥人都覺得在墨西哥開分公司是個好主意。

⑧ **nonsense** [`nɑnsɛns] (*n.*) 胡說；廢話

例 I don't think it's nonsense. It's a good idea, if you ask me.

我不覺得那是胡說八道，倒覺得那是個好主意。

⑨ **fishing** [`fɪʃɪŋ] (*n.*) 釣魚

例 My dad and I used to go fishing together when I was young.

我小時候，我爸都會和我一起去釣魚。

⑩ **stuck** [stʌk] (*adj.*) 被困住的

例 Why do we have to be stuck inside on such a beautiful day?

天氣這麼好，我們為什麼要待在家裡不出去？

## 🖈 進階字彙

### 描述工作的方式

| | | | |
|---|---|---|---|
| **interesting** | [ˋɪntrɪstɪŋ] | (adj.) | 有趣的 |
| **boring** | [ˋborɪŋ] | (adj.) | 無聊的 |
| **dull** | [dʌl] | (adj.) | 單調乏味的;令人生厭的 |
| **difficult** | [ˋdɪfəˌkʌlt] | (adj.) | 艱難的 |
| **repetitive** | [rɪˋpɛtɪtɪv] | (adj.) | 反覆的 |

### 與退休有關的詞彙

| | | | |
|---|---|---|---|
| **elderly** | [ˋɛldəlɪ] | (adj.) | 年長的 |
| **pension** | [ˋpɛnʃən] | (n.) | 退休金;養老撫恤金 |
| **severance package** | [ˋsɛvərəns ˋpækɪdʒ] | (n.) | 遣散費 |
| **early retirement** | [ˋɜlɪ rɪˋtaɪrmənt] | (n.) | 提早退休 |
| **step down** | [stɛpˋdaun] | (v.) | 退位;離職 |

在美國,人們不一定要在什麼時候退休,只要他們想,隨時都可以退休。而且他們退休後,會從事很多活動來豐富生活,像是一些戶外休閒活動,如釣魚、健行、槌球,或是室內的活動如打牌、下午茶等,甚至也有人再進入學校繼續學習,所以退休人們的生活其實是很多采多姿的。

# ✎ Exercises 動手做

請從以下字彙中，挑出正確的單字填入空格內。

| retire | fishing | partner | |
|---|---|---|---|
| stuck | nonsense | spare time | challenging |

1. This lake is great for _____.

2. Being a doctor must be a _____ job.

3. I'd like to take you to dinner. When do you usually have _____?

4. Don't listen to her. She's talking _____.

5. At what age do you plan to _____?

1. 這個湖是很棒的釣魚地點。
2. 當醫生一定是個很有挑戰性的工作。
3. 我想帶你去吃晚餐，你通常什麼時候有空？
4. 別聽她的，她在胡說八道。
5. 你計畫要在幾歲退休呢？

解答　1. fishing　2. challenging　3. spare time　4. nonsense　5. retire

**A** 選一最適合的字完成下列句子

1. After working at the company for five years, Hector finally received a _____ to supervisor.
   - (A) correspondence
   - (B) work force
   - (C) customer
   - (D) promotion

2. I like to read mystery novels in my _____.
   - (A) spare time
   - (B) experience
   - (C) competition
   - (D) effort

3. The company is working hard to _____ its retiring plant manager.
   - (A) relax
   - (B) hesitate
   - (C) offer
   - (D) replace

4. Don't you think it's _____ that all the windows in the house are open?
   - (A) dissatisfied
   - (B) strange
   - (C) superior
   - (D) challenging

5. Sales people who beat their sales targets will receive a salary _____.
   - (A) transfer
   - (B) know-how
   - (C) bonus
   - (D) respect

將下列空格填入最適合的單字

It's not easy for a company to ____(1)____ its current CEO with a new one. Hopefully the current CEO will willingly ____(2)____. Typically he or she is offered a large ____(3)____ to make the decision easy. But if the person isn't willing to step down, it may be necessary to force him or her out, through the actions of the Board of Directors and possibly a vote of no-confidence by shareholders.

Once the position is vacant, the next task is to find a suitable replacement. A CEO needs to be many things for a company. He or she must have the business ____(4)____ to steer the company in the right direction. A CEO is also a company's main spokesperson, standing before the press, shareholders, and other big players in the industry. It's a ____(5)____ job, and few people are qualified for the task. No wonder salaries for CEOs are often millions of dollars per year.

1. (A) underestimate (B) replace    (C) complain       (D) deserve
2. (A) retire          (B) introduce (C) compare        (D) realize
3. (A) competitor      (B) effort     (C) work force     (D) bonus
4. (A) know-how        (B) nonsense (C) correspondence (D) promotion
5. (A) blunt           (B) disastrous (C) challenging    (D) stuck

**A** 1. D   2. A   3. D   4. B   5. C

翻譯

1. 在這家公司工作了五年之後，海特終於獲得晉升為主管。
2. 我閒暇之餘喜歡閱讀推理小說。
3. 公司正努力要找人替代退休的廠長。
4. 整間屋子的窗戶都是打開的，你不覺得很奇怪嗎？
5. 能超越銷售目標的推銷員會得到額外獎金。

**B** 1. B   2. A   3. D   4. A   5. C

翻譯

對公司來說，要讓新的人取代現任的執行長並不是一件容易的事。現任的執行長若願意退休自然是再好不過。一般而言，為了容易達成這項決議，他會得到一大筆的津貼。但是如果這個人不願意下台，或許就有必要迫使他離開，由董事會來採取行動或也可能是由股東進行不信任投票。

一旦這個職務空了出來，接下來的任務就是要找適合的替代人選。執行長在一家公司中扮演多重的角色。他必須具備商業知識以引領公司走向正確的方向。執行長也是公司主要的發言人，他要面對媒體、股東和業界其他的大老。這是個很有挑戰性的工作，只有少數的人有資格擔此重任。難怪執行長通常有好幾百萬的年薪。

# 「閱讀」是增加字彙的最佳途徑

增加字彙的最佳方法就是閱讀，將閱讀英文列為你每週例行公事的重要事項，那麼，你將發現不僅字彙基礎會獲得改善，連口說、聽力、及其他技巧也將有所增進。

## ☑ 為何閱讀很重要呢？

閱讀最主要的好處，就是能讓你在不同情境的上下文中大量接觸到字彙。諸如在故事、文章、新聞報導等題材中，都會有大量的句型及詞類變化，所以如果你讀的故事或文章較長，而且是同位作者寫的，你就會發現作者會一再使用某些字和片語，一再接觸到相同的字彙可建立你對字的認識度，並讓你能更容易的記住這些字彙。

讓我告訴你一個有關閱讀重要性的真實故事。當我在哈佛念研究所時，我修了一門現代中國文學的課程，所有的課程資料，包括故事、文章、電影及演講稿都是用中文寫成的，你可以想像，對我而言這是個很大的挑戰，除了每週都要閱讀很多中文文章外，我也必須寫短篇的論文作業，那真是非常難啊！

沒錯，修課期間發生了件有趣的事喔！雖然我那時在美國，大部分時間說的是英文，但我的中文，包括口說跟寫作的技巧，居然都大有進步呢！主要原因就是閱讀，讀課堂上的教材、查生字、按進度閱讀都只是基本功，除此之外，我還將常碰到並覺得有用的單字寫在我的記事本中，經常地複習這些字。可以確定的是，大量的練習

作業讓我有機會能接觸到有用的字彙跟片語。

念完研究所後，我來到台灣，大家都知道，畢業後的生活與在學校是截然不同的，因為工作我又再度的忙碌起來，也沒有花時間來閱讀中文了，猜猜怎麼著，即便我每天都在說中文，我的中文居然變差了！怎麼會這樣呢？這都是因為我的閱讀量減少了。與人交談時，我用的字彙都差不多，也很少從所交談的人身上學到新的字彙跟片語，而我也無法享受到像在哈佛時，那種能學到大量字彙跟片語的樂趣了。這個故事想說的是，不論你身處何方，也無論你是否是在英語系國家，固定的閱讀習慣絕對可以增進你的字彙能力及一般的英語能力。

## ☑ 該閱讀那些題材？

建議你找自己感興趣的東西來讀，如果要強迫自己去閱讀不感興趣的文章，那麼進步的空間可能就有限，所以，如果你對科學很感興趣，那麼盡可能地閱讀科學雜誌、或是科學相關的非小說類作品。如果你從事國際貿易，並希望多了解這個領域，那麼就可以多讀些市面上暢銷的的商業雜誌。或者，如果你喜歡讀推理小說，市面上也有很多英文小說可供選擇。你所選的閱讀素材不一定要跟你的工作領域相關，只要能養成固定閱讀英文的習慣，必能改善你整體的英文能力。

## ☑ 閱讀量應該要多少呢？

如果可能的話，試著養成一週兩小時的閱讀習慣，兩小時的時間能

讓你完成一些事。首先，要能維持對常用英語句型的熟悉度，接著，你會接觸到許多常用的英文字彙，這會對你有所幫助，因為同時也能複習到一些最近剛學的單字，最後你當然也會遇到一些新的單字跟片語，你可以將它們記在你的筆記中，匯整成你個人的英語字彙本。

當然，如果行有餘力可以多閱讀的話，那就更好了！不過，如果你行程已經滿檔的話，也不用太勉強，因為你反而會感到疲憊與透支。要謹記在心的是你應該要讀你所愛，並把固定的英語閱讀習慣視為一種樂趣，而不是痛苦的責任。

我個人喜歡讀文學，像是現代短篇小說，當代小說，以及大量的古典文學名著。我也時常喜歡閱讀詩集，所以，當我想要學中文，西班牙文或法文時，我就會找一些文學作品來讀，或者，我也可能選擇戲劇，閱讀劇本是增進口語能力最好的方法，此外，戲劇通常也很有趣。

# Chapter 5
# 商務、金融與消費

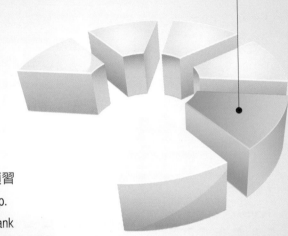

英語學習專欄 **5**
學習和練習字彙的更多秘訣

## Preview 字彙預習

| | |
|---|---|
| approved | 被認可的；經檢驗而核可的 |
| bill | 帳單 |
| cash register | 收銀機 |
| cashier | 收銀員 |
| change | 零錢；找的錢 |
| classical music | 古典樂 |
| copy | 份數 |
| discount | 折扣 |
| gift | 禮物 |
| hip hop | 嘻哈音樂 |
| hope | 希望 |
| inflation | 通貨膨脹 |
| jazz | 爵士樂 |
| pop | 流行樂 |
| receipt | 收據；發票 |
| rock and roll | 搖滾樂 |
| shelf | 架子 |
| tax | 稅金／對⋯⋯課稅 |
| total | 總金額；合計 |
| wrap | 包裝 |

找零篇

*Mandy has finished shopping. She takes her items to the register.*

Cashier: Will that be all?

Mandy: That will do it. Can you wrap the red shirt up? It's a gift.

Cashier: No problem. Your total is $73.45.

Mandy: Wow. The way inflation is going, I won't be able to buy anything in a few years. OK, here's 80.

Cashier: Thanks. $6.55 is your change. And, here's your receipt.

翻譯

*曼蒂挑完要買的東西，帶著這些東西到收銀檯。*

收銀員：全部就這些嗎？

曼蒂　：就是這些了，你能幫我把這件紅色襯衫**包起來**嗎？那是個**禮物**。

收銀員：沒問題，總共是七十三塊四五。

曼蒂　：哇！如果**通貨膨脹**持續下去的話，再過幾年我就再也不能買東西了。　好吧，這裡是八十塊。

收銀員：謝謝，找你的**零錢**六塊五五，還有，這是你的**發票**。

結帳篇

*Randy is paying for his items at a music store.*

Randy: I was hoping to get two copies of this Ricky Martin CD, but there was only one on the shelf.

Cashier: We can order it for you if you want.

Randy: No, I need it today. I'll take these CDs for now. Here's my credit card.

Cashier: Thank you, sir ... I'm sorry, your card was not approved.

Randy: What! I thought I paid the bill on time. All right, I'll have to write you a check.

翻譯

*唱片行裡，藍迪買了一些東西，正要結帳。*

藍迪　：我**希望**能買到這兩**張**瑞奇‧馬汀的這片 CD，不過**架上**只有一張。

收銀員：如果你還想要的話，我們可以幫你訂。

藍迪　：不用了，我今天就要，我先拿這些 CD 好了，這是我的信用卡。

收銀員：謝謝您，先生……很抱歉，您的卡不**能用**。

藍迪　：什麼！我都有準時付**帳單**啊。好吧，看來我得開張支票給你了。

① **wrap** [ræp] (*v.*) 包裝

例 Mrs. Warren wraps up presents beautifully.
華倫太太能把禮物包裝地很漂亮。

② **gift** [gɪft] (*n.*) 禮物

例 Don't tell me you're giving him the same gift as I am!
別告訴我你跟我要送給他的禮物是一樣的。

③ **inflation** [ɪnˋfleʃən] (*n.*) 通貨膨脹

例 The newspaper said inflation last year was just over four percent.
報上說去年的通貨膨脹率剛好超過百分之四。

④ **change** [tʃendʒ] (*n.*) 零錢；找的錢

例 I think you gave me the wrong change.
我想你找給我的零錢是錯的。

⑤ **receipt** [rɪˋsit] (*n.*) 收據；發票

例 Save your receipt in case you need to return the sweater.
保留你的發票以防你要退還那件毛衣。

⑥ **hope** [hop] (*v.*) 希望

例 I hope they have the CD player I'm looking for.
我希望他們有我要找的 CD 播放器。

⑦ **copy** [ˋkɑpɪ] (*n.*) 份數

例 We put out 10 copies this morning, and we were sold out by noon.
今天早上我們放出十份，到中午就賣完了。

⑧ **shelf** [ʃɛlf] (*n.*) 架子

例 Can you help me get something from the top shelf?
你可以幫我從最上面的架子拿個東西嗎？

⑨ **approved** [əˋpruvd] (*adj.*) 被認可的；經檢驗而核可的

例 The loan application was approved by the bank.
銀行已經核准貸款申請了。

⑩ **bill** [bɪl] (*n.*) 帳單

例 I get more bills than letters every month.
每個月我所收到的帳單比信件還要多。

## 🔖 進階字彙

| | | |
|---|---|---|
| **cashier** | [kæ`ʃɪr] (*n.*) 收銀員 | |
| **cash register** | [kæʃ rɛdʒɪstə] (*n.*) 收銀機 | |
| **discount** | [`dɪskaʊnt] (*n.*) 折扣 | |
| **total** | [`totl̩] (*n.*) 總金額；合計 | |
| **tax** | [tæks] (*n./v.*) 稅金／對……課稅 | |

| | | |
|---|---|---|
| **rock and roll** | [`rɑk ɛn `rol] (*n.*) 搖滾樂 | |
| **jazz** | [dʒæz] (*n.*) 爵士樂 | |
| **classical music** | [`klæsɪkl̩] (*n.*) 古典樂 | |
| **pop** | [pɑp] (*n.*) 流行樂 | |
| **hip hop** | [`hɪp `hɑp] (*n.*) 嘻哈音樂 | |

文化總匯

在美國的商店或餐廳裡要結帳時，人們都會用信用卡或支票付帳，除非金額很小才會付現；美國人並不習慣隨身攜帶大量現金。在美國的店裡消費都要加付營業稅，各州規定的營業稅額都不大相同，大都在消費額的百分之六至九之間；若是美國政府規定不必納稅的項目，就不用加營業稅。

# ✎ Exercises 動手做

請從以下字彙中，挑出正確的單字填入空格內。

| inflation | approved | receipt | |
|-----------|----------|---------|------|
| copy | gift | bill | wrap |

1. I was going to pay the phone _____ yesterday, but I forgot to.

2. Can I borrow your _____ of John Grisham's new book?

3. What _____ are you going to buy your dad for Father's Day?

4. During the Christmas buying season, many stores hire someone just to _____ items for customers.

5. Here's the _____ for this jacket, which I bought last week.

**翻譯**

1. 我昨天本來要付電話帳單,但是我忘了。
2. 我可以跟你借你那本約翰·格里斯罕的新書嗎?
3. 你父親節要買什麼禮物送你爸?
4. 在耶誕節購物期間,很多店會加僱一個人專門為顧客包裝。
5. 這是我上週買的外套的發票。

解答 1. bill 2. copy 3. gift 4. wrap 5. receipt

## Preview 字彙預習

| | |
|---|---|
| **account** | 帳戶 |
| **apply** | 申請 |
| **ATM card** | 金融卡；提款卡 |
| **balance** | 餘額；結餘 |
| **branch** | 分行 |
| **checking account** | 支票帳戶 |
| **chop** | 印章 |
| **deposit** | 存款 |
| **endorse** | （在票據）背面簽名背書 |
| **hassle** | 麻煩；問題 |
| **maintain** | 維持；保持 |
| **minor** | 次要的；不重要的 |
| **overdrawn** | 透支 |
| **passbook** | 銀行存摺 |
| **PIN code** | 密碼 |
| **savings account** | 存款帳戶 |
| **service charge** | 手續費 |
| **signature** | 簽名 |
| **teller** | 銀行出納員 |
| **withdraw** | 提款 |

## Andrew's 精選對話

### 開戶篇

*Mr. Lyons wants to open a new account.*

Bank staff: What kind of account do you want to open?

Mr. Lyons: Probably a checking account. Is there a monthly service charge?

Bank staff: Not if you maintain a balance of $5,000.

Mr. Lyons: That shouldn't be a problem.

Bank staff: Great. First, I need you to fill out this form.

### 翻譯

*里昂先生想開一個新的帳戶。*

銀行職員：你想開辦什麼帳戶呢？

里昂先生：應該是支票帳戶吧，每個月需要付手續費嗎？

銀行職員：如果帳戶裡保持有五千塊錢的餘額就不用。

里昂先生：那應該不成問題。

銀行職員：很好，首先，我要請您填這張表。

提款篇

*Mrs. Stone needs a new ATM card.*

Mrs. Stone: I tried to use my ATM card yesterday, but it didn't work.

Bank staff: Is the card for your savings account?

Mrs. Stone: Yes, it is. It's not going to be a big hassle to apply for a new one, is it?

Bank staff: Not at all. It's a minor problem. We can get you a new card within a few days.

Mrs. Stone: Good, because I do most of my banking through those machines.

翻譯

*史東太太需要一張新的金融卡。*

史東太太：我昨天試著使用我的**金融卡**，但是它沒辦法作業。

銀行職員：這是您**存款帳戶**的卡嗎？

史東太太：是的，要**申請**一張新卡不會很**麻煩**吧，會嗎？

銀行職員：一點也不麻煩，那個問題**不大**，我們可以在幾天內發一張新卡給您。

史東太太：那就好，因為我幾乎都是用那些提款機來管理我的財務的。

① **account** [əˋkaʊnt] (*n.*) 帳戶

例 I have accounts at several different banks.
我在好幾家不同的銀行都有帳戶。

② **checking account** [ˋtʃɛkɪŋ əˋkaʊnt] (*n.*) 支票帳戶

例 The problem with checking accounts is they usually don't
pay any interest.
支票帳戶有個問題就是：它們通常都不付利息的。

③ **service charge** [ˋsɜvɪs ˋtʃɑrdʒ] (*n.*) 手續費

例 That type of account has a monthly service charge of $5.
那種帳戶每個月要付五塊錢的手續費。

④ **maintain** [menˋten] (*v.*) 維持；保持

例 I try to maintain a balance of $1,000 or so in my checking
account.
我試著讓支票帳戶的結餘能保持在一千塊左右。

⑤ **balance** [ˋbæləns] (*n.*) 餘額；結餘

例 Your current balance is $3,450.
你目前的餘額是三千四百五十元。

⑥ **ATM card** [ˋeˋtiˋ em ˋkɑrd] (*n.*) 金融卡；提款卡

例 ATM cards can be used to withdraw cash from machines all around the world.
金融卡可以在全世界的提款機提款。

⑦ **savings account** [ˋsevɪŋz əˋkaʊnt] (*n.*) 存款帳戶

例 Your mother and I think it's time you had your own savings account.
你媽和我覺得該是你擁有自己的存款帳戶的時候了。

⑧ **hassle** [ˋhæsl] (*n.*) 麻煩；問題

例 Since I lost my wallet, it's been a big hassle reapplying for all my bank cards and credit cards.
自從我掉了錢包後，重新申請所有的銀行用卡及信用卡一直是個大麻煩。

⑨ **apply** [əˋplaɪ] (*v.*) 申請

例 You have to be at least 18 years old to apply for a credit card.
你最少要滿十八歲才能申請信用卡。

⑩ **minor** [ˋmaɪnɚ] (*adj.*) 次要的；不重要的

例 It was just a minor accident. There's no need to apologize.
那只是個小意外，沒必要道歉的。

## 🔖 進階字彙

金融相關字 1

| | | |
|---|---|---|
| **deposit** | [dɪ`pɑzɪt] | (n./v.) 存款 |
| **withdraw** | [wɪð`drɔ] | (v.) 提款 |
| **teller** | [`tɛlɚ] | (n.) 銀行出納員 |
| **PIN code** | [`pɪn `kod] | (n.) 密碼 |
| **branch** | [bræntʃ] | (n.) 分行 |

金融相關字 2

| | | |
|---|---|---|
| **overdrawn** | [`ovɚ`drɔn] | (adj.) 透支 |
| **passbook** | [`pæs͵buk] | (n.) 銀行存摺 |
| **signature** | [`sɪgnətʃɚ] | (n.) 簽名 |
| **endorse** | [ɪn`dɔrs] | (v.)（在票據）背面簽名背書 |
| **chop** | [tʃɑp] | (n.) 印章 |

文化總匯

美國人如果需要任何的金融服務，絕大多數都會使用自動提款機。美國所有銀行設置的自動提款機都可以提款、存款、存支票、轉帳、支付帳單等，但是一天內所能提領的金額最多只能有幾百塊美金；還有一些特別的提款機可以直接買賣股票，這種提款機只有在大銀行才會提供。

# ✏ Exercises 動手做

請從以下字彙中，挑出正確的單字填入空格內。

| apply | checking account | maintain | |
|---|---|---|---|
| ATM card | hassle | minor | balance |

1. Remembering the PIN numbers for all my ATM cards is a
   _____.

2. My _____ lets me write 10 checks for free every
   month.

3. It only takes five minutes if you want to _____
   for a credit card.

4. I don't know why my boss got so mad. The mistake I made
   was really _____.

5. I get charged a small fee if I use my _____ at
   another bank's machine.

1. 要記得我所有金融卡的密碼真是麻煩。

2. 我的支票帳戶可以讓我每個月開出十張免收手續費的票子。

3. 如果你想辦信用卡的話，只要花五分鐘就可以了。

4. 我不知道老闆為什麼這麼生氣，我只不過犯了個小小的錯誤而已。

5. 如果我在別家銀行的機器使用我的金融卡，我就要付一點手續費。

解答 1. hassle　2. checking account　3. apply　4. minor　5. ATM card

## Preview 字彙預習

| | |
|---|---|
| **arrive** | 到達 |
| **available** | 有空的；可用的 |
| **bell boy** | 旅館大廳幫忙提行李的人員 |
| **bridal suite** | 蜜月套房 |
| **computer** | 電腦 |
| **concierge** | 旅館服務臺職員 |
| **corner suite** | 邊間套房 |
| **deluxe room** | 豪華客房 |
| **double** | 單床雙人房 |
| **executive suite** | 高級套房 |
| **hotel manager** | 飯店經理 |
| **luxurious** | 豪華的；奢侈的 |
| **maid** | 女僕 |
| **porter** | 提行李的腳伕 |
| **reservation** | 預訂；預約 |
| **single room** | 單人房 |
| **spacious** | 寬敞的；廣闊的 |
| **standard room** | 一般客房 |
| **twin** | 雙床雙人房 |
| **view** | 景觀 |

**櫃檯詢問篇**

*Mrs. Asherton walks into a hotel to ask about a room.*

Clerk: Good afternoon, miss. How may I help you?

Mrs. Asherton: I need a single room. Do you have any available?

Clerk: Yes, we do. Would that be a standard or a deluxe room? As you can see from these pictures, the deluxe rooms are more spacious.

Mrs. Asherton: I don't need anything luxurious. A standard room will be fine.

**翻譯**

*艾雪頓太太走進一家飯店詢問住房。*

職員　　　：午安，女士，我能幫您什麼忙嗎？

艾雪頓太太：我需要一間**單人房**，有**空**房間嗎？

職員　　　：有的，要**一般客房**或**豪華客房**呢？就如您在這些照片上看到的，豪華客房比較**寬敞**。

艾雪頓太太：我不需要太**豪華**的東西，一間標準客房就好了。

電話訂房篇

*Mr. Bower calls a hotel to reserve a room.*

Mr. Bower: Hi, I'd like to make a reservation.

Clerk: I'd be glad to help you with that. What dates will you be staying?

Mr. Bower: I'll arrive in town on the 16th, and I'll stay for three nights.

Clerk: Let me check the computer... Yes, we do have rooms available.

Mr. Bower: Good. I'd like a room with a nice view.

翻譯

*鮑爾先生打電話給某飯店預定房間。*

鮑爾先生：嗨，我想**預訂**一個房間。

職員　　：我很高興能幫您忙，您的住房日期會是哪幾天？

鮑爾先生：我會在十六號**抵達**城裡，並且在那裡待三個晚上。

職員　　：讓我查一下**電腦**……沒問題，我們有空房。

鮑爾先生：那好，我要一個**景觀**不錯的房間。

---

① **single room** [`sɪŋgl `rum] (*n.*) 單人房

例 I'm sorry, we don't have any single rooms open.
我很抱歉，我們沒有空的單人房。

---

② **available** [ə`veləbl] (*adj.*) 有空的；可用的

例 There are plenty of rooms available.
還有很多空房間。

---

③ **standard room** [`stændəd `rum] (*n.*) 一般客房

例 Standard rooms all have a TV, but no window.
一般客房都有電視，不過沒窗戶。

---

④ **deluxe room** [dɪ`lʌks `rum] (*n.*) 豪華客房

例 Our deluxe rooms have a large bathroom and a mini-bar.
我們的豪華客房都有一個大型浴室還有迷你吧台。

---

⑤ **spacious** [`speʃəs] (*adj.*) 寬敞的；廣闊的

例 The hotel's lobby was so spacious that several hundred
people could fit inside.
這個飯店的大廳好寬敞，裡面可以容納好幾百人。

---

⑥ **luxurious** [lʌgˈʒurɪəs] *(adj.)* 豪華的；奢侈的

例 For once, let's stay at a luxurious hotel during our vacation.

就一次，我們渡假時住豪華飯店吧。

⑦ **reservation** [ˌrɛzəˈveʃən] *(n.)* 預訂；預約

例 I was able to make my reservation on the Internet.

我可以在網路上預訂。

⑧ **arrive** [əˈraɪv] *(v.)* 到達

例 Call me as soon as you arrive.

你一到就給我個電話。

⑨ **computer** [kəmˈpjutə] *(n.)* 電腦

例 Our computers are down, so we're doing everything by hand.

我們的電腦當機了，所以任何事都得手動。

⑩ **view** [vju] *(n.)* 景觀

例 What a lovely view! You can see all the way to the ocean from here.

好棒的景觀喔！你可以從這裡一路看到海。

## 🔍 進階字彙

### 飯店房間種類

**twin**　　　　　　　[twɪn] (*n.*) 雙床雙人房

**double**　　　　　　[dʌbl] (*n.*) 單床雙人房

**corner suite**　　　['kɔrnɚ 'swit] (*n.*) 邊間套房

**bridal suite**　　　['braɪdl 'swit] (*n.*) 蜜月套房

**executive suite**　[ɪg'zɛkjutɪv 'swit] (*n.*) 高級套房

### 飯店職員

**bell boy**　　　　　['bɛl 'bɔɪ] (*n.*) 旅館大廳幫忙提行李的人員

**porter**　　　　　　['portɚ] (*n.*) 提行李的腳伕

**maid**　　　　　　　[med] (*n.*) 女僕

**concierge**　　　　[ˌkɑnsɪ'ɛrʒ] (*n.*) 旅館服務臺職員

**hotel manager**　　[ho'tɛl 'mænɪdʒɚ] (*n.*) 飯店經理

文化總匯

美國有幾種形式的旅館，在大城市裡或觀光地區，通常叫做飯店 (Hotel)；如果是在公路上的，就叫做汽車旅館 (Motel)，它們在房間前面提供停車位；而最便宜的住房則是宿舍型的旅店 (Hostel)，需跟別人同住，旅店裡不供餐，但是有廚房，可以自己煮東西吃。

# ✏ Exercises 動手做

請從以下字彙中，挑出正確的單字填入空格內。

| luxurious | reservation | standard room | |
|-----------|-------------|---------------|---------|
| spacious | arrive | available | computer |

1. Do you have any rooms _____ on August the 12th?

2. We should _____ at 11:00 at night.

3. I know it's not very _____, but it's big enough for me.

4. I just need your name and telephone number, and your _____ will be completed.

5. Your room has a piano in it? Now that's _____.

1. 你們八月十二日有空房間嗎？

2. 我們應該會在晚上十一點到達。

3. 我知道那不是很寬敞，不過對我來說夠大了。

4. 我只要你的姓名和電話號碼，就可以完成預約了。

5. 你的房裡有鋼琴？還真豪華呢。

解答 **1.** available **2.** arrive **3.** spacious **4.** reservation **5.** luxurious

# At the Post Office

郵局裡

## Preview 字彙預習

| | |
|---|---|
| **afford** | 付得起；買得起 |
| **airmail** | 航空郵件 |
| **customs declaration form** | 海關申報單 |
| **express delivery** | 快遞 |
| **first class** | 優先投遞郵件 |
| **insure** | 投保 |
| **insured** | 已經投保的 |
| **letter** | 信件 |
| **necessary** | 必要的；必須的 |
| **overnight mail** | 隔夜寄達的郵件 |
| **package** | 包裹 |
| **parcel** | 包裹 |
| **postcard** | 明信片 |
| **printed matter** | 印刷品 |
| **priority mail** | 優先寄達郵件 |
| **reasonable** | 合理的；公道的 |
| **registered mail** | 掛號郵件 |
| **sea mail** | 海運郵件 |
| **surface mail** | 水陸郵件 |
| **weigh** | 秤重 |

寄包裹篇

*A woman wants to send a package to Australia.*

Woman: How much will this cost to send?

Worker: By surface mail or airmail?

Woman: Airmail.

Worker: Let me weigh it... It will cost $17.00. And you need to fill out this customs declaration form. Do you want to insure it?

Woman: No, that won't be necessary.

翻譯

*有位女士想要寄包裹到澳洲去。*

女士　　：寄這個要多少錢？

工作人員：要寄**水陸郵件**或是**航空郵件**？

女士　　：**航空郵件**。

工作人員：我來幫它**秤重**一下……要花十七塊錢，還有，你必須填好這個**海關申報單**，這個包裹要**投保**嗎？

女士　　：不用了，沒這個**必要**。

寄信篇

*A man has a letter to send to Italy.*

Man: What's the fastest way to send this to Italy?

Worker: You could send it by overnight mail, but it's expensive - almost $35.

Man: I can't afford that. Any other options?

Worker: Express delivery, which costs $3.50 and takes four to seven days.

Man: That's far more reasonable.

翻譯

*有位男士要寄信到義大利。*

男士　　：寄信到義大利用什麼方式最快？

工作人員：你可以用**隔夜寄達**的方式，不過那很貴──將近三十五塊錢。

男士　　：那我**付**不起，還有其他的選擇嗎？

工作人員：**快遞**，那個要花三塊半，四到七天的時間就可寄到。

男士　　：**合理**多了。

① **surface mail** [ˋsɝfɪs ˋmel] (n.) 水陸郵件

例 How long will it take to send this by surface mail?

這個用水陸郵件寄要多久才會到？

② **airmail** [ˋɛrˌmel] (n.) 航空郵件

例 At the post office, tell them you want it sent by airmail.

到了郵局，告訴他們你這個要寄航空郵件。

③ **weigh** [ˋwe] (v.) 秤重

例 When I weighed the box, I couldn't believe how heavy it was.

我秤這個箱子時，真不敢相信會那麼重。

④ **customs declaration form** [ˋcʌstəmz ˌdɛkləˋreʃən fɔrm] (n.) 海關申報單

例 Most customs declaration forms are green, and they're written in English and French.

大部分的海關申報單是綠色的，而且是用英文和法文寫的。

⑤ **insure** [ɪnˋʃur] (v.) 投保

例 You can insure the parcel for up to $2,000.

你可以替這個包裹加保，保金可以高達兩千元。

⑥ **necessary** [ˈnɛsə ˌsɛrɪ] (*adj.*) 必要的；必須的

例 It isn't necessary to put an airmail sticker on the envelope.

信封上不一定要貼航空郵件的標籤貼紙。

⑦ **overnight mail** [ˈovəˈnaɪt ˈmel] (*n.*) 隔夜寄達的郵件

例 This has to be in Los Angeles tomorrow, so I'll have to send it by overnight mail.

這個必須在明天到達洛杉磯，所以我得用隔夜寄達的方式寄出。

⑧ **afford** [əˈfɔrd] (*v.*) 付得起；買得起

例 I want to buy that old stamp for my collection, but I can't afford it.

我想為我自己的收藏購買那張舊郵票，不過我買不起。

⑨ **express delivery** [ɪkˈsprɛs dɪˈlɪvərɪ] (*n.*) 快遞

例 I'm sorry, we don't offer express delivery service to that country.

我很抱歉，我們沒有提供送到那個國家的快遞服務。

⑩ **reasonable** [ˈriznəbl̩] (*adj.*) 合理的；公道的

例 If you don't think Federal Express has reasonable prices, you can try UPS.

如果你覺得聯邦快遞的價格不合理，你可以試試 UPS。

## 📌 進階字彙

### 郵寄物件

| | |
|---|---|
| **letter** | [ˋlɛtə] (*n.*) 信件 |
| **package** | [ˋpækɪdʒ] (*n.*) 包裹 |
| **parcel** | [ˋpɑrsl] (*n.*) 包裹 |
| **postcard** | [ˋpostˌkɑrd] (*n.*) 明信片 |
| **printed matter** | [ˋprɪntəd ˋmætə] (*n.*) 印刷品 |

### 其他郵寄方式

| | |
|---|---|
| **first class** | [ˋfɜst ˋklæs] (*n.*) 優先投遞郵件 |
| **priority mail** | [praɪˋɔrətɪ ˋmel] (*n.*) 優先寄達郵件 |
| **registered mail** | [ˋrɛdʒɪstəd ˋmel] (*n.*) 掛號郵件 |
| **insured** | [ɪnˋʃurd] (*adj.*) 已經投保的 |
| **sea mail** | [ˋsi ˋmel] (*n.*) 海運郵件 |

美國的郵局受理信件與包裹的寄送服務，也賣郵票，但是沒有提供像台灣的郵局帳戶、郵政保險等的金融業務。美國家庭門前的郵箱雖然是屋主購買的，但裡面的空間是屬於美國政府的，所以不能隨意把東西放到郵箱裡面，除非屋主豎起郵箱的小旗子，示意裡面有待寄的信件。

# ✎ Exercises 動手做

請從以下字彙中，挑出正確的單字填入空格內。

| reasonable | customs declaration form | insures | |
|---|---|---|---|
| necessary | surface mail | weigh | afford |

1. Our company _____ all the packages it sends, in case anything is damaged along the way.

2. That's a _____ price. OK, I'll take it.

3. It will take at least two months by _____.

4. You didn't fill out the contents' value on the _____.

5. It's only $2.50. I think you can _____ that.

翻譯

1. 我們公司將所有寄出的包裹投了保，以防有東西在路上受損。

2. 那個價格很合理。好吧，我買了。

3. 水陸郵件最少要花兩個月的時間。

4. 你沒有填好海關聲明表單上內容物價值的部分。

5. 這個只有兩塊半，我想你買得起的。

解答 1. insures   2. reasonable   3. surface mail
4. customs declaration form   5. afford

## Preview 字彙預習

| | |
|---|---|
| **blueprint** | 藍圖 |
| **commercial** | 商業的 |
| **complicated** | 複雜的；難懂的 |
| **develop** | 開發 |
| **encouraged** | 受到鼓舞的 |
| **forbidden** | 禁止的 |
| **illegal** | 非法的 |
| **inquire** | 詢問；查詢 |
| **inspection** | 檢驗；審視 |
| **law** | 法律 |
| **legal** | 合法的；正當的 |
| **outline** | 列出要點 |
| **pamphlet** | 小冊子 |
| **permit** | 允許；核准 |
| **permitted** | 准許的；許可的 |
| **property** | 產業；房地產 |
| **regulation** | 規章；管理；條例 |
| **retail store** | 零售商店 |
| **violation** | 違規 |
| **zone** | 地區；地帶 |

**零售業篇**

*Frederick wants to open an art supply store.*

Frederick: I'd like to inquire about getting a business license for a retail store.

Clerk: What did you need to know?

Frederick: Are there any laws about where I can open it?

Clerk: It has to be in a commercial zone. We have books that list where each of those zones are.

Frederick: I'd like to have a look at those, please.

**翻譯**

*費德瑞克想開一家美術用品店。*

費德瑞克：我想**詢問**有關取得**零售店**營業執照的事情。

職員　　：你想知道些什麼呢？

費德瑞克：有**法律**規定我能開在哪裡嗎？

職員　　：必須開在**商業區**。我們有書冊列出每個商業區的所在位置。

費德瑞克：我想看看那些書，麻煩你。

房地產篇

*Flora asks about building a house.*

Flora: I want to develop my property by building a house on it. So, where do I start?

Clerk: First, you need to fill out these forms.

Flora: Is the whole thing going to be complicated?

Clerk: I'm afraid so. Here's a pamphlet that outlines the process.

Flora: It's 30 pages long! This is going to be a lot of work.

翻譯

*芙蘿拉詢問關於蓋房子的事。*

芙蘿拉：我想蓋棟房子來**開發**我的**房地產**，我該從何處著手？

職員　：首先，你要先填好這些表單。

芙蘿拉：這整件事會很**複雜**嗎？

職員　：恐怕是，這裡有個**小冊子**，裡面**列出**了所有的程序。

芙蘿拉：有三十頁耶！看來得花很多工夫了。

① **inquire** [ɪnˋkwaɪr] (*v.*) 詢問；查詢

例 We're here to inquire about your ad in the newspaper.
我們來這裡是要詢問您在報紙上登的廣告。

② **retail store** [ˋritel ˋstor] (*n.*) 零售商店

例 Running a retail store is a lot of work.
經營零售店很辛苦。

③ **law** [lɔ] (*n.*) 法律

例 How is anyone supposed to understand all these laws?
誰會懂這些法律嘛？

④ **commercial** [kəˋmɝʃəl] (*adj.*) 商業的

例 The office complex is located in the city's biggest commercial district.
這個商業中心座落在城裡最大的商業特區內。

⑤ **zone** [zon] (*n.*) 地區；地帶

例 They told me the place I wanted to rent is not in a commercial zone.
他們說我想租的地方不在商業區內。

6) **develop** [dɪˋvɛləp] (*v.*) 開發

例 The city spent millions of dollars developing its poor neighborhoods.

這個城市花了好幾百萬來開發其貧窮的區域。

7) **property** [ˋprɑpətɪ] (*n.*) 產業；房地產

例 This property is one of the most expensive in the state.

這房地產是這個州裡最昂貴的之一。

8) **complicated** [ˋkɑmpləˌketɪd] (*adj.*) 複雜的；難懂的

例 After reading the guidelines, Dorin realized they weren't very complicated.

在讀過概要後，朵琳發現它們並不難懂。

9) **pamphlet** [ˋpæmflɪt] (*n.*) 小冊子

例 Hand me one of those pamphlets.

從那些小冊子裡拿一本給我。

10) **outline** [ˋautˌlaɪn] (*v.*) 列出要點

例 What I need is a manual that outlines the procedure step by step.

我所需要的是一本列出逐步程序的手冊。

## 🖈 進階字彙

**regulation** [ˌrɛɡjəˈleʃən] (*n.*) 規章；管理；條例

**inspection** [ɪnˈspɛkʃən] (*n.*) 檢驗；審視

**permit** [pəˈmɪt] (*n.*) 允許；核准

**blueprint** [ˈbluˌprɪnt] (*n.*) 藍圖

**violation** [ˌvaɪəˈleʃən] (*n.*) 違規

**形容能做和不能做的事**

**legal** [ˈliɡl̩] (*adj.*) 合法的；正當的

**illegal** [ɪˈliɡl̩] (*adj.*) 非法的

**permitted** [pəˈmɪtɪd] (*adj.*) 准許的；許可的

**forbidden** [fəˈbɪdn̩] (*adj.*) 禁止的

**encouraged** [ɪnˈkɝɪdʒd] (*adj.*) 受到鼓舞的

文化總匯

在美國要蓋一棟新房子，過程是很繁複的，因為每州、郡都有不同的建築規範，建築上的任一細節都要經過核可；例如建築藍圖、施工設計圖、建材……等等，還要考慮其設計是否符合當地的景觀。如果當地的社區發展組織也有建築方面的規範，也必須要符合該社區的要求。

# ✐ Exercises 動手做

請從以下字彙中，挑出正確的單字填入空格內。

| develop | commercial | complicated | |
|---------|-----------|-------------|-----|
| property | inquired | pamphlet | law |

1. I can't believe it's against the _____ to build a fourth story on my own house!

2. I _____ about the cost of getting a permit, but the person didn't know.

3. I heard they're going to _____ that land into a huge shopping center.

4. This is just too _____. I'll never figure it out.

5. Can you believe it? The city wants to build a freeway right through the center of my _____!

1. 我真無法相信在我自己的房子上蓋第四層樓是違法的。

2. 我去問了許可證的費用,不過那人不知道。

3. 我聽說他們要將那塊地開發為一間大型購物中心。

4. 這太複雜了,我永遠也猜不出來。

5. 你相信嗎?市政府想蓋的那條高速公路直接穿過我的房地產中央!

解答　1. law　2. inquired　3. develop　4. complicated　5. property

# Exercises 單字總復習 🔍 ✏

**A** 選一最適合的字完成下列句子

1. Many hotels allow guests to make _____ over the Internet.
   - (A) hassles
   - (B) laws
   - (C) computers
   - (D) reservations

2. High _____ rates can do a lot of damage to an economy.
   - (A) checking account
   - (B) inflation
   - (C) pamphlet
   - (D) standard room

3. Because Dave's monthly salary was low, his loan application was not _____.
   - (A) approved
   - (B) complicated
   - (C) spacious
   - (D) available

4. _____ is the cheapest way to send something, but it takes a long time.
   - (A) Express delivery
   - (B) Airmail
   - (C) Overnight mail
   - (D) Surface mail

5. On a(n) _____, you write down the goods you are bringing into a country and their value.
   - (A) savings account
   - (B) service charge
   - (C) customs declaration form
   - (D) ATM card

Modern hotels have a variety of rooms and services to meet the needs of a range of guests. Business travelers typically stay in standard rooms, though they may stay in a ___(1)___ if they're executives. These travelers often require a good business services center, with fax machines, ___(2)___, and so on.

Tourists, depending on the amount of money they can ___(3)___, may stay in any of the hotel's rooms. Tourists are usually interested in a hotel's recreational services, such as its spa, swimming pool, and exercise room.

Finally, there are rare visitors, such as heads of state, royalty, and celebrities. They choose only the best hotels with the most ___(4)___ suites. The suite will need to be ___(5)___ enough for an office, living room, and perhaps a small kitchen. It is in fact like a small apartment and may be the only part of the hotel the guest ever sees.

1. (A) deluxe room (B) retail store (C) reservation (D) property
2. (A) zones (B) outlines (C) computers (D) shelves
3. (A) insure (B) wrap (C) inquire (D) afford
4. (A) available (B) approved (C) luxurious (D) commercial
5. (A) spacious (B) complicated (C) reasonable (D) minor

**A** 1. D　2. B　3. A　4. D　5. C

翻譯

1. 許多飯店都可以讓客人上網訂房。
2. 高度的通貨膨脹率會對經濟造成很大的傷害。
3. 因為戴夫的月薪很低，所以他的貸款申請沒有被核准。
4. 水陸郵件是最便宜的寄件方式，但是會花上很久的時間。
5. 在海關申報單上，你要填上你攜帶入境的商品以及它們的價值。

**B** 1. A　2. C　3. D　4. C　5. A

翻譯

現代化的飯店提供多樣化的房間和服務來滿足不同客層的需求。商務客人通常會住一般客房，不過如果是公司主管的話，也許就會住豪華房。這些旅客往往需要一個好的商務服務中心，提供他們傳真機、電腦等等。

觀光客則依他們能負擔的金額高低不同，可能會住飯店的任何一種房間。觀光客通常對飯店內的休閒設施極感興趣，像是水療中心、游泳池和健身房。

最後是貴賓級的房客，例如國家元首、皇室成員以及名人。他們只選擇頂級飯店中最豪華的套房。套房必須夠寬敞，要有辦公室、客廳，或許還能有個小廚房。事實上那就像一間小型的公寓，而且可能是該房客在飯店中唯一會見到的部份。

# 更多學習和練習字彙的秘訣

## ☑ 流行娛樂

在讀過本書的單字後，可以觀察這些字彙在母語人士的娛樂節目中所佔比例，如果可能的話，將整個句子寫下來，這會提供你更多有用的上下文，進而讓你對這些字有更深的了解。

## ☑ 網際網路

網路是學習新字以及讓你應用在本書中所學字彙的最佳途徑，大家在網路上的用字都比較不正式且較口語化，差不多介於口語和書面的英語間，就像是電子郵件的書寫方式。

你可以瀏覽一些討論區和網站，或是到聊天室與母語人士聊天，在聊天室裡，可看到英文在不同情境下的使用狀況，也剛好可以趁機運用所學的字，看看別人的反應。你不用在聊天室裡說出自己的名字，也不需要與人面對面，這無疑是探索語言的最佳機會。

需要注意的是，在聊天室中，要表現的自然一點，使用你最熟悉的英文，也不必一直想讓別人留下深刻的印象，同時，如果你不了解他人的意思，那也沒關係，畢竟聊天室裡通常都有很多人，你不一定要回覆所有的談話。

## ☑ 找出中文裡相對應的說法

連結所學單字與自己的母語是很有趣的學習方式，並非所有的英文

單字都可在母語中找到相對應的字，但大部分的字彙是有可能的，所以盡可能的去找出相近的字吧！

## ☑ 主動進行寫作練習

要成為成功的語言學習者，關鍵就在於主動，除了大量閱讀外，寫作的練習也很重要，藉由寫下自己的英文文章，就多增加了你對英文的了解，這樣可以幫助你整合新的字彙、片語、句型等，並打好英文的基礎，信不信由你，這個練習除了能增進你的寫作技巧外，也會對你的聽力、口說，閱讀技巧有很大的幫助，這種有創造力的活動，除了可加強你對字彙的了解外，也可同時幫助你記憶。

## ☑ 利用單字創造簡短對話

就學單字的情況而言，我會建議為每個單字寫個六至八行的簡短對話，並準備筆記本把這些對話記下來，對話不需是很精心設計的，重點是，不要擔心寫的句子不夠完美，這不是像在學校中所寫的文章，會被嚴格的教授打分數，也不會有人責備你將標點符號放錯地方，更重要的是，這樣的書寫方式並不是要讓你堆積一些無可挑剔的文章或是對話，關鍵是要讓你成為有創造力的語言學習者，並加深你對原文文章的認識。

## ☑ 不要過於擔心犯錯

此外，我還要跟你們分享一個小秘訣，即使是英語人士所寫的英文也無法完全正確無誤。沒錯，英語人士從國中甚至到研究所，都不斷地在犯錯，但他們在寫作時，並不會擔心是否每個細節都正確無

誤，所以你也不需為此操心，不過，對於一些較為嚴肅的文章形式，如商業書信和論文，建議你還是要做校訂，而且是越正確越好。

這裡有個簡單的對話範例，你可以試著用一些單字來寫寫看。

Karen:    Do you know about the big baseball game this weekend?

George: Sure. I want to go, since the <u>stadium</u> is near my house.

Karen:    I was thinking about going too, but it's going to be so <u>crowded</u>.

George: That's what I'm worried about. Also, the <u>weather</u> might be bad.

Karen:    Hmm, maybe we can watch it at a sports bar.

George: Good idea!

凱倫：你知道這個週末有場重要的棒球比賽嗎？
喬治：當然知道啦！我要去看，反正體育館就在我家附近。
凱倫：我也想去，不過我想應該會很擠吧！
喬治：我也正在擔心這個。而且，天氣可能也會不好。
凱倫：嗯！我們乾脆到有轉播球賽的酒吧裡去看好了。
喬治：好主意耶！

你也可以將本對話中的單字列出來，如下：

- **stadium**   體育館
- **crowded**   擁擠的
- **weather**   天氣

## ☑ 將單字實際運用在生活中

或是，在每隔一段時間後，如幾週或幾個月，你可以試著將本書的單字實際的應用在生活中。每當你應用了一個單字，就在本書最後的索引頁中作個記號。如果有你特別喜歡的單字，更要經常的使用它，用的越多次，就越能運用自如，也越容易記起來。

而要使會話能多樣化呈現，就要廣泛的使用情境與功能。例如，某天你可能會寫出工作情境下的對話。接著，可以試著寫出國旅遊時的對話，或讓對話中人物扮演購物者的角色。而你可能也會想將語言的功能整合到會話當中，例如向某人問路，購買東西，請求說明等等。寫的範圍是沒有任何限制的，只要運用你的想像力，就會很有趣！

另外，你也可以嘗試用英文寫日記。在每一篇中，以使用本書所學到的二至三個單字為目標。或者，你可以做些不一樣的東西，如寫個小故事。不要擔心自己無法成為下個莎士比亞，其他人是不會讀到你的故事的，除非你到處給人家看，但那一定也很好玩！最主要的是用英文做些好玩的事，也可以順便達到練習的效果，不是很好嗎？只要能自在地使用所學過的單字，就能夠增強你對字的認識與使用它的能力了。

# Chapter 6
# 交通、旅遊導覽、運動休閒

## Preview 字彙預習

| | |
|---|---|
| basketball | 籃球 |
| batter | 打擊手 |
| coach | 教練 |
| cricket | 板球 |
| crowd | 人群 |
| embarrassing | 難堪的；丟人的 |
| first place | 排名第一；領先 |
| football | 美式足球 |
| league | 聯盟 |
| optimistic | 樂觀的 |
| pitcher | 投手 |
| playoffs | 決賽；季後賽；延長賽 |
| referee | 裁判 |
| rush | 趕緊；急促 |
| score | 分數／得分 |
| season | 球季 |
| soccer | 足球 |
| stadium | 體育場；球場 |
| tennis | 網球 |
| victory | 勝利 |

# Andrew's 精選對話 　　　　　　　　　　　　🔊 MP3 49

**輸球篇**

*Kevin's favorite team is losing.*

Kevin: This is embarrassing. My team's getting killed.

Manny: They're up against the first place team. What do you expect?

Kevin: For starters, the batters could start doing their job.

Manny: Not against Pedro Santos. He's one of the best pitchers in the league.

Kevin: I know, I know.

**翻譯**

*凱文最喜歡的球隊快輸了。*

凱文：真**難堪**啊，我最喜歡的球隊被痛宰了。

曼尼：他們對打的是**排名第一**的球隊啊，你還能期望什麼？

凱文：首先，**打擊手**就可以開始盡他們的責任啊。

曼尼：面對沛卓‧山多斯，他們是是沒辦法的，他可是**聯盟**中最佳的**投手**之一。

凱文：我知道，我知道。

244

**比賽結束篇**

*Towards the end of the game, Kevin wants to leave.*

Kevin:　Let's get out of here.

Manny:　What's the rush?

Kevin:　The stadium's almost full today. I want to leave before the rest of the crowd.

Manny:　Don't you want to watch the end of the game? There's still time for a come-from-behind victory.

Kevin:　Hah! You're more optimistic than I am. Really, I don't think they have a chance.

**翻譯**

*比賽快要結束了，凱文想先離開。*

凱文：我們走吧。

曼尼：幹嘛這麼急？

凱文：今天**體育館**裡幾乎客滿了，我想比其他人早一步離開。

曼尼：你不想看比賽結果嗎？還有反敗為**勝**的時間啊。

凱文：哈！你比我還**樂天**吶，說真的，我不覺得他們有機會。

① **embarrassing** [ɪmˋbærəsɪŋ] (*adj.*) 難堪的；丟人的

例 That play was so bad it was embarrassing.
那個打擊動作好爛，真丟人。

---

② **first place** [ˋfɜst ˋples] (*n.*) 排名第一；領先

例 The L.A. Lakers have been in the first place all this year.
洛杉磯湖人隊這一整年一直保持領先。

---

③ **batter** [ˋbætɚ] (*n.*) 打擊手

例 We need some batters who can knock the ball out of the park.
我們需要些可以把球擊出場外的打擊手。

---

④ **pitcher** [ˋpɪtʃɚ] (*n.*) 投手

例 That was close! The pitcher almost hit the guy in the face with a fastball.
真接近啊！投手投出的快速球幾乎打到那傢伙的臉。

---

⑤ **league** [lig] (*n.*) 聯盟

例 There are 35 teams in the league.
聯盟裡共有三十五支球隊。

⑥ **rush** [rʌʃ] (*n.*) 趕緊;急促

例 Johnson needs to take his time, instead of always taking his shots in a rush.

強森需要慢慢來,而不要老是急急忙忙地行動。

⑦ **stadium** [ˋstedɪəm] (*n.*) 體育場;球場

例 The new stadium is much bigger than the old one.

新的體育館比舊的要大很多。

⑧ **crowd** [kraʊd] (*n.*) 人群

例 Nick doesn't like being around crowds, so he prefers watching ball games at home on TV.

尼克不喜歡跟人擠來擠去,所以他比較喜歡在家看電視轉播的球賽。

⑨ **victory** [ˋvɪktrɪ] (*n.*) 勝利

例 If our football team gets one more victory, we'll break the school record.

如果我們的足球隊再贏一場球,就會打破學校紀錄。

⑩ **optimistic** [ˌɑptəˋmɪstɪk] (*adj.*) 樂觀的

例 It's hard to be optimistic when you've lost eight games in a row.

如果你連輸八場球賽,你是很難樂觀起來的。

**運動種類**

| | | |
|---|---|---|
| **football** | [ˋfʊtˏbɔl] | (n.) 美式足球 |
| **basketball** | [ˋbæskɪtˏbɔl] | (n.) 籃球 |
| **tennis** | [ˋtɛnɪs] | (n.) 網球 |
| **soccer** | [ˋsɑkɚ] | (n.) 足球 |
| **cricket** | [ˋkrɪkɪt] | (n.) 板球 |

**運動賽事常用詞語**

| | | |
|---|---|---|
| **referee** | [ˏrɛfəˋri] | (n.) 裁判 |
| **coach** | [kotʃ] | (n.) 教練 |
| **score** | [skor] | (n./v.) 分數／得分 |
| **season** | [ˋsizn̩] | (n.) 球季 |
| **playoffs** | [ˋpleˏɔfs] | (n.) 決賽；季後賽；延長賽 |

**文化總匯**

在美國，棒球場的觀眾有時會故意吆喝、咒罵來激怒裁判或球員，大多時候他們都不予理會，但也曾經有球員被激怒而跑到觀眾席跟觀眾打架的事。有些觀眾會帶棒球手套來看球，若有球飛出場外，他們可以接下這些球，因為球場外的球是屬於觀眾的。

## ✏ Exercises 動手做

請從以下字彙中，挑出正確的單字填入空格內。

| embarrassing | optimistic | first place | |
|---|---|---|---|
| league | rush | crowd | batter |

1. The _____ is going to expand to 42 teams next year.

2. The _____ cheered wildly when Mark McGwire hit a home run.

3. That _____ has enough power to hit the ball out of the stadium.

4. For the first time in 20 years, we finished in _____.

5. Our coach said we should be _____ no matter how bad we're losing.

1. 聯盟在明年會擴充到四十二隊。

2. 當馬克・馬奎爾擊出全壘打時，群眾們熱烈地歡呼。

3. 那個打擊者有足夠的力氣把球擊出體育場外。

4. 二十年來第一次，我們以第一名收場。

5. 教練說，不管我們輸得多慘，都應該樂觀些。

解答 1. league　2. crowd　3. batter　4. first place　5. optimistic

## Preview 字彙預習

| | |
|---|---|
| **abroad** | 往（在）國外 |
| **Australia** | 澳洲 |
| **beach** | 沙灘；海灘 |
| **book** | 訂票；訂位；預訂 |
| **convince** | 說服；使信服；使確信 |
| **critical** | 要緊的；關鍵的；危急的 |
| **Egypt** | 埃及 |
| **England** | 英國 |
| **France** | 法國 |
| **Japan** | 日本 |
| **London** | 倫敦 |
| **mortgage** | 房貸 |
| **New York** | 紐約 |
| **Paris** | 巴黎 |
| **perfect** | 完美的；最適當的 |
| **settle** | 決定；解決 |
| **Sydney** | 雪梨 |
| **Tokyo** | 東京 |
| **travel agent** | 旅遊業者 |
| **weird** | 奇怪的；詭異的 |

暑假計劃篇

*Mark and Lewis are making summer vacation plans.*

Lewis: We need to hurry up and book a plane ticket. What's it going to be—Greece or France?

Mark: Let's think this through. They've both got good beaches.

Lewis: Which is the most critical thing. The food is supposed to be good in France.

Mark: Good, but expensive. Also, remember Jack said he went there, and he ate some weird stuff.

Lewis: No weird food for me, thanks. That settles it. Let's go to Greece.

翻譯

*馬克和路易斯正在決定暑期渡假計劃。*

路易斯：我們必須趕快**訂機票**，目的地是希臘還是法國？

馬克　：我們先想清楚，它們都有很棒的**海灘**。

路易斯：這是**最重要的**。法國的食物應該很好吃。

馬克　：是很好，但是很貴，還有，你記得傑克說過他去那裡吃到很**奇怪的**東西吧。

路易斯：我可不要奇怪的食物，謝謝。那就**決定**了，我們去希臘吧。

渡假計劃實現篇

*Mara and Jerry are finally going on vacation.*

Mara: Jerry, we've been talking about traveling abroad for so long. I really, really want to see Japan.

Jerry: Can't we make it next year?

Mara: But this is the perfect year. The kids are at college, the mortgage is paid off, and we have money in the bank.

Jerry: Now that you put it that way, you're right. All right, you've convinced me. Pack your bags, Mara, we're going to Japan!

Mara: Yes! I'm calling a travel agent right now to ask about tickets.

翻譯

*瑪拉和傑利終於要去渡假了。*

瑪拉：傑利，我們說要**出國**玩已經說好久了，我真的真的很想去日本看看。

傑利：我們不能明年去嗎？

瑪拉：不過，今年**最好**啊，孩子們都上大學了，**房貸**也都繳清了，而且我們銀行裡還有存款。

傑利：既然妳都這麼說了，說得對，好吧，妳**說服**我了，去打包妳的行李，瑪拉，我們要去日本了！

瑪拉：太棒了！我現在就打電話給**旅遊業者**問機票的事。

① **book** [buk] (*v.*) 訂票；訂位；預訂

例 Hector usually books his plane ticket one week before he goes on vacation.

海克特通常都在要去渡假的前一個禮拜訂機票。

② **beach** [bitʃ] (*n.*) 沙灘；海灘

例 I never dreamed the beach would be so crowded in the middle of the week.

我從來也想不到在非週末的時候，海邊也會這麼擁擠。

③ **critical** [ˋkrɪtɪkl] (*adj.*) 要緊的；關鍵的；危急的

例 It's critical that you keep your passport safe at all times.

隨時把你的護照放在安全的地方是很要緊的事。

④ **weird** [wɪrd] (*adj.*) 奇怪的；詭異的

例 I understand it was some kind of traditional dance. I still thought it was weird.

我了解那是某種傳統舞蹈，不過我還是覺得它很詭異。

⑤ **settle** [ˋsɛtl] (*v.*) 決定；解決

例 Let's settle tomorrow's plan during dinner tonight.

我們今天晚餐時就來決定明天的計劃吧。

⑥ **abroad** [ə`brɔd] (*adv.*) 往 ( 在 ) 國外

例 One hundred years ago, few people had the chance to travel abroad.

一百年前，很少人有機會到國外旅行。

⑦ **perfect** [`pɜfɪkt] (*adj.*) 完美的；最適當的

例 The sky is clear, and there's a cool breeze. It's perfect weather for a hike.

天空很清澈，還有涼風吹，這是最適合健行的天氣。

⑧ **mortgage** [`mɔrgɪdʒ] (*n.*) 房貸

例 If you don't repay your mortgage on time, the bank may repossess your house.

如果你不準時償還房貸，銀行是可以收回你的房子的。

⑨ **convince** [kən`vɪns] (*v.*) 說服；使信服；使確信

例 Maybe we can convince Mom to take us to Universal Studios this year.

也許我們可以說服老媽今年帶我們去環球影城玩。

⑩ **travel agent** [`trævl `edʒənt] (*n.*) 旅遊業者

例 A good travel agent can save you a lot of money on plane tickets.

好的旅遊業者能幫你省很多機票錢。

## 🔖 進階字彙

**France**      [fræns] (*n.*) 法國
**England**      [ˋɪŋglənd] (*n.*) 英國
**Japan**      [dʒəˋpæn] (*n.*) 日本
**Egypt**      [ˋidʒɪpt] (*n.*) 埃及
**Australia**      [ɔˋstreljə] (*n.*) 澳洲

受歡迎的旅遊城市

**Paris**      [ˋpærɪs] (*n.*) 巴黎
**London**      [ˋlʌndən] (*n.*) 倫敦
**New York**      [nuˋjɔrk] (*n.*) 紐約
**Tokyo**      [ˋtokɪo] (*n.*) 東京
**Sydney**      [ˋsɪdnɪ] (*n.*) 雪梨

文化總匯

在美國，一些受到公司倚重的專業人士，是很少有機會去渡假或旅行的，雖然公司每年會給予大概七到十天左右的年假，但公事繁忙，也不一定有機會利用這些年假。有小孩的人，通常都會儘量在小孩放暑假時，安排年假，全家出遊。在歐洲，因為政府的規定，專業人士的假期都有二到六個禮拜之久。

# ✎ Exercises 動手做

請從以下字彙中，挑出正確的單字填入空格內。

| mortgage | travel agent | convince | |
|----------|--------------|----------|--------|
| beach | abroad | settle | perfect |

1. She goes _____ on business several times a year.

2. I'll ask my _____ if there are any flights leaving on the 25th.

3. No matter what you say, you won't _____ me to agree with you.

4. I think Paris would be the _____ place for a honeymoon.

5. Here's a picture of me sitting on the _____ and watching the waves roll by.

1. 她每年因公出國好幾次。

2. 我會問我的旅遊業者看二十五號有沒有班機。

3. 不管你說什麼,你都不能說服我同意你的看法。

4. 我想巴黎會是蜜月的最佳地點。

5. 這張照片是我坐在沙灘上看著潮來潮往。

解答 1. abroad  2. travel agent  3. convince  4. perfect  5. beach

## Preview 字彙預習

| | |
|---|---|
| **alight** | 下車 |
| **board** | 登上（火車） |
| **cabin** | 客艙；小屋 |
| **conductor** | 火車隨車服務員；車掌 |
| **depart** | 出發；離開 |
| **driver** | 司機 |
| **fare** | 車資 |
| **journey** | 旅程 |
| **leg room** | 伸腳的空間 |
| **observation car** | 觀景車 |
| **passenger** | 乘客 |
| **purchase** | 購買 |
| **recline** | 斜臥 |
| **relief** | 鬆了口氣；一大解脫 |
| **rest stop** | 休息站 |
| **restaurant car** | 餐車 |
| **schedule** | 時刻表 |
| **station** | 車站；站 |
| **stretch** | 伸展 |
| **vending machine** | 販賣機 |

**搭火車篇**

*At a train station, a customer asks about tickets.*

Customer: Is there a direct train to Detroit?

Ticket seller: Yes, we have trains departing every three hours.

Customer: How long is the trip?

Ticket seller: I'll check the schedule... you're looking at a seven-hour journey.

Customer: In that case, I'd like a cabin so I can sleep on the way.

**翻譯**

*在火車站，有個客人詢問車票的事。*

客人　：有直達底特律的火車嗎？

售票員：有的，我們每三個小時**發**一班車。

客人　：要多久時間才會到？

售票員：我查一下**時刻表**……**旅程**總共要花七小時。

客人　：在那種情況下，我想要個**臥艙**，這樣我就可以在路上睡一下。

## 搭公車篇

*At a bus station, a customer asks about tickets.*

Customer: When's the next bus for Detroit?

Ticket seller: 11:34. Would you like to purchase a ticket?

Customer: Yes, please. How many rest stops are there along the way?

Ticket seller: The bus stops at several stations on the way to Detroit. You'll have a few minutes to stretch your legs or get something from a vending machine.

Customer: That's a relief. I was worried I'd be sitting on the bus all day.

## 翻譯

*在巴士站，有個客人詢問車票的事。*

客人 ：下一班到底特律的巴士是什麼時候？

售票員：十一點三十四分。你想**買票**嗎？

客人 ：是的，麻煩你。一路上有多少個**休息站**？

售票員：巴士在前往底特律的途中會停好幾**站**，你會有一些時間**伸伸腿**或是去**販賣機**買些東西。

客人 ：那真讓人**鬆一口氣**，我還擔心我可能得在巴士上坐一整天呢。

① **depart** [dɪˋpɑrt] (v.) 出發；離開

例 Due to the bad weather, the bus will not depart on time.
由於天氣很差，巴士不會準時出發。

② **schedule** [ˋskɛdʒul] (n.) 時刻表

例 Free copies of the bus schedule are available at the ticket counter.
免費的巴士時刻表可以在售票櫃檯取得。

③ **journey** [ˋdʒɝnɪ] (n.) 旅程

例 It's a three-hour journey, so you might want to bring something to read.
那是趟三小時的旅程，你也許會想帶個什麼在路上閱讀。

④ **cabin** [ˋkæbɪn] (n.) 客艙；小屋

例 All three of us can share one cabin.
我們三個可以共用一間小屋。

⑤ **purchase** [ˋpɝtʃəs] (v.) 購買

例 If you purchase your ticket one month in advance, you'll get a 15-percent discount.
如果你提前一個月買票，可享八五折優待。

⑥ **rest stop** [ˋrɛst ˋstɑp] (*n.*) 休息站

例 I'll ask the driver how long we have until the next rest stop.

我會問司機我們還要多久才到下個休息站。

⑦ **station** [ˋsteʃən] (*n.*) 車站；站

例 The station is open 24 hours a day.

這個車站二十四小時全天營業。

⑧ **stretch** [strɛtʃ] (*v.*) 伸展

例 You'll feel better after you stretch your legs.

你伸伸腿後會覺得比較好。

⑨ **vending machine** [ˋvɛndɪŋ məˋʃin] (*n.*) 販賣機

例 The vending machine only takes coins, not bills.

販賣機只收硬幣，不收鈔票。

⑩ **relief** [rɪˋlif] (*n.*) 鬆了口氣；一大解脫

例 What a relief to see the sky clearing after it rained so long.

下雨下了這麼久後，能看到清澈的天空，真是一大解脫。

## 🔑 進階字彙

### 鐵道旅行字彙

| | |
|---|---|
| **board** | [bord] (*v.*) 登上（火車） |
| **alight** | [əˋlaɪt] (*v.*) 下車 |
| **conductor** | [kənˋdʌktə] (*n.*) 火車隨車服務員；車掌 |
| **observation car** | [ˌɑbzɚˋveʃən ˋkɑr] (*n.*) 觀景車 |
| **restaurant car** | [ˋrɛstərənt ˋkɑr] (*n.*) 餐車 |

### 巴士旅行字彙

| | |
|---|---|
| **driver** | [ˋdraɪvə] (*n.*) 司機 |
| **passenger** | [ˋpæsṇdʒə] (*n.*) 乘客 |
| **recline** | [rɪˋklaɪn] (*v.*) 斜臥 |
| **leg room** | [ˋlɛg ˋrum] (*n.*) 伸腳的空間 |
| **fare** | [fɛr] (*n.*) 車資 |

文化總匯

美國最大的鐵路客運公司是 Amtrak。很多人喜歡花兩三天的時間搭火車，他們的目的不是為了去某個地方，而是為了欣賞鐵路沿線的美麗景致。美國最大的巴士營運是 Greyhound，行駛路線涵蓋全美國。大城市與大城市間的距離雖遠，但票價不貴。很少人選擇搭巴士進行長程旅行，因為車裡的座位不大，長久搭乘會很不舒服。

# ✏ Exercises 動手做

請從以下字彙中，挑出正確的單字填入空格內。

| vending machine | purchase | relief | |
|---|---|---|---|
| stretch | schedule | journey | depart |

1. Let's _____ our tickets before the ticket window closes.

2. The _____ says the last bus leaves at 11:45.

3. The _____ took my money but didn't give me my drink.

4. It's important to _____ a while before playing sports.

5. How long will the _____ last?

1. 我們在售票窗口關閉前買票吧。

2. 時刻表上說最後一班公車在十一點四十五分離開。

3. 販賣機吞了我的錢卻沒給我飲料。

4. 在運動前先伸展一下很重要。

5. 這趟旅行會花多久的時間？

解答 1. purchase　2. schedule　3. vending machine　4. stretch　5. journey

## Preview 字彙預習

| | |
|---|---|
| **airline** | 航空公司 |
| **aisle seat** | 靠走道座位 |
| **beverage** | 飲料 |
| **blanket** | 毛毯；被子 |
| **business class** | 商務艙 |
| **comfortable** | 舒適的；自在的 |
| **considerate** | 體貼的；考慮周到的 |
| **economy class** | 經濟艙 |
| **famous** | 著名的 |
| **fight attendant** | 空服員 |
| **flight** | 飛行；航班 |
| **freezing** | 冰凍的；極冷的 |
| **layover** | 中途停留 |
| **one-way** | 單程票 |
| **pleasure** | 高興；意願 |
| **reconfirm** | 再確定（飛機座位） |
| **relative** | 親戚 |
| **round-trip** | 來回票 |
| **waiting list** | 候補名單 |
| **window seat** | 靠窗座位 |

**咖啡或茶**

*A passenger calls the flight attendant over.*

Attendant: Yes, miss?

Passenger: I'd like another blanket. It's freezing in here.

Attendant: I'll get you one. Would you like a hot beverage — coffee or tea maybe?

Passenger: Why, yes, that would warm me up. That's very considerate of you.

Attendant: It's my pleasure.

**翻譯**

*有個乘客呼叫空服員過來。*

空服員：有什麼事嗎，小姐？

乘客　：我還想多要一條**毯子**，這裡**好冷**。

空服員：我會拿一條給您，您想要熱的**飲料**嗎，也許來個咖啡或是茶？

乘客　：喔，好啊，那可以讓我暖和起來，你真的**很體貼**。

空服員：我很**高興**能為你服務。

**飛機餐**

*Two passengers are talking to each other.*

Man: Is this your first time visiting Dallas?

Woman: Yes, I'm going to see some relatives.

Man: That's good. It's been a comfortable flight, but the food, well ...

Woman: I know what you mean. This airline isn't exactly famous for its food.

Man: Oh, yes it is. It's famous for being bad!

**翻譯**

*兩位乘客在聊天。*

男：這是你第一次造訪達拉斯嗎？

女：是啊，我要去那裡看一些**親戚**。

男：那不錯啊，這是趟**舒適的飛行**，只不過這個食物嘛，嗯……

女：我知道你的意思，這個**航空**公司並非以它提供的食物**聞名**。

男：喔，它是，它是以提供差勁的食物聞名的！

① **blanket** [ˈblæŋkɪt] (*n.*) 毛毯；被子

　　例 There are extra blankets in the closet.
　　衣櫃裡有多的被子。

---

② **freezing** [ˈfrizɪŋ] (*adj.*) 冰凍的；極冷的

　　例 It's freezing in this room. I'll turn on the heater.
　　這房間冷死人了，我要去開暖器。

---

③ **beverage** [ˈbɛvərɪdʒ] (*n.*) 飲料

　　例 What kind of beverage would you like?
　　你想喝什麼飲料？

---

④ **considerate** [kənˈsɪdərɪt] (*adj.*) 體貼的；考慮周到的

　　例 Helping that elderly woman cross the street was very
　　considerate of you.
　　你幫助那位老婦人過街真的好體貼喔。

---

⑤ **pleasure** [ˈplɛʒɚ] (*n.*) 高興；意願

　　例 A: Can you help me carry this suitcase?
　　B: My pleasure.
　　A: 您能幫我拿這個行李箱嗎？
　　B: 我很樂意。

⑥ **relative** [ˈrɛlətɪv] (*n.*) 親戚

例 Most of my relatives live in the south of the country.
我大多數的親戚住在我國南方。

⑦ **comfortable** [ˈkʌmfətəbl] (*adj.*) 舒適的；自在的

例 It's hard to stay comfortable while sitting in an airplane for 11 hours.
在飛機裡坐十一個小時實在很難保持舒適。

⑧ **flight** [flaɪt] (*n.*) 飛行；航班

例 The flight was delayed due to heavy rain.
這個班機延誤是因為大雨的關係。

⑨ **airline** [ˈɛrˌlaɪn] (*n.*) 航空公司

例 Because of the long layover, the airline provided passengers with free hotel rooms.
因為中途停留太久，航空公司提供旅客們免費的飯店住房。

⑩ **famous** [ˈfeməs] (*adj.*) 著名的

例 I saw a famous person at the airport!
我在機場看到一個名人！

## 🖈 進階字彙

### 機艙常用字

| | | |
|---|---|---|
| **window seat** | [ˈwɪndo ˈsit] (n.) | 靠窗座位 |
| **aisle seat** | [ˈaɪl ˈsit] (n.) | 靠走道座位 |
| **economy class** | [ɪˈkɑnəmɪ ˈklæs] (n.) | 經濟艙 |
| **business class** | [ˈbɪznɪs ˈklæs] (n.) | 商務艙 |
| **fight attendant** | [ˈflaɪt əˈtɛndənt] (n.) | 空服員 |

### 機票相關字

| | | |
|---|---|---|
| **one-way** | [ˈwʌn ˈwe] (n.) | 單程票 |
| **round-trip** | [ˈraʊnd ˈtrɪp] (n.) | 來回票 |
| **layover** | [ˈleˌovə] (n.) | 中途停留 |
| **waiting list** | [ˈwetɪŋ ˈlɪst] (n.) | 候補名單 |
| **reconfirm** | [ˌrikənˈfɝm] (v.) | 再確定（飛機座位） |

文化總匯

美國境內機場最忙碌的時候是耶誕節和感恩節的前兩天，那時會有幾百萬甚至千萬的人趕著搭飛機回家過節，機票的費用在這個時候也相對地提高。暑假是旅遊的旺季，機票的費用最貴。美國的航空公司有個現象，就是當其中一家調漲或調降票價時，其他航空公司也會一起同步調價。

## ✎ Exercises 動手做

請從以下字彙中，挑出正確的單字填入空格內。

| considerate | beverage | blanket | |
|---|---|---|---|
| relatives | flight | freezing | airlines |

1. Do all of your _____ come from Hong Kong?

2. It's _____. Can you close the window?

3. If you're thirsty, I can bring you a _____.

4. Tell me your _____ number so I can meet you at the airport.

5. Many _____ offer good discounts in the wintertime.

1. 你所有的親戚都從香港來嗎?
2. 好冷啊,你可以把窗戶關上嗎?
3. 你口渴的話,我可以幫你帶杯飲料。
4. 告訴我你的班機號碼,這樣我就可以到機場接你。
5. 很多航空公司在冬季時會提供優惠折扣。

解答 1. relatives   2. freezing   3. beverage   4. flight   5. airlines

## Preview 字彙預習

| | |
|---|---|
| **amusement park** | 遊樂園 |
| **attend** | 參加；出席 |
| **attraction** | 吸引人的東西；吸引力 |
| **cathedral** | 教堂 |
| **concert** | 音樂會；演奏會；演唱會 |
| **consider** | 考慮 |
| **cultural** | 文化的；人文的 |
| **entertainment** | 娛樂；消遣 |
| **fair** | 展覽會；廟會；市集 |
| **festival** | 節慶；慶典 |
| **monument** | 紀念碑；紀念建築物 |
| **musical** | 歌舞劇 |
| **national park** | 國家公園 |
| **opera** | 歌劇 |
| **parliament** | 議會；國會 |
| **play** | 戲劇 |
| **temple** | 寺廟 |
| **vicinity** | 附近地區 |
| **wonder** | 想知道；不明白；納悶 |
| **zoo** | 動物園 |

**觀光客篇**

*In London, a tourist asks for help at an information booth.*

Worker: Good morning, sir. How may I help you?

Tourist: I was wondering what local attractions are worth seeing. I only have a few hours to spend.

Worker: You might consider visiting Westminster Cathedral. It's in the vicinity of Big Ben and the parliament.

Tourist: Can I see all that in a few hours?

Worker: I'd say so, yes.

**翻譯**

*在倫敦，有位觀光客在資訊站尋求協助。*

工作人員：早安，先生，我能幫你忙嗎？

觀光客 ：我想知道此地有哪些景點值得一看，我只有幾個小時的時間。

工作人員：你可以考慮參觀西敏寺，那就在大笨鐘和英國國會的附近。

觀光客 ：我能在幾個小時內逛完那裡所有的景點嗎？

工作人員：我想應該可以。

商務旅遊篇

*A business traveler in New York enters a visitor information center.*

Traveler: While I'm here, I'd like to attend a concert or another cultural event. How can I find out about those sorts of things?

Worker: Your best source would be "Time Out." It's a weekly entertainment guide.

Traveler: Where can I get a copy?

Worker: Most bookstores sell them. Try the Barnes and Noble down the road.

Traveler: I'll give them a try. Thanks.

翻譯

*一個到紐約的商業客進入了一家旅客諮詢中心。*

旅行者 ：我在這停留的期間，想去**參加**個**音樂會**或是其他的**文化**活動，我要怎麼找到這類的資訊？

工作人員：《休閒時間》會是你最好的資料來源，那是本**娛樂**導覽週刊。

旅行者 ：哪裡可以買到？

工作人員：大部分的書店都有賣，試試這條路上的 Barnes and Nobles 書店吧。

旅行者 ：我會去那裡看看的，謝謝。

① **wonder** [ˋwʌndə] (v.) 想知道；不明白；納悶

例 I wonder if that musical is any good.
我想知道那個歌舞劇好不好看。

② **attraction** [əˋtrækʃən] (n.) 吸引人的東西；吸引力

例 This city has enough attractions to keep us busy all week.
這個都市有足夠的景點讓我們整個禮拜都忙著參觀。

③ **consider** [kənˋsɪdə] (v.) 考慮

例 Did you consider the amount of time it will take to drive there?
你有考慮過開車到那裡所要花費的時間嗎？

④ **cathedral** [kəˋθidrəl] (n.) 教堂

例 The Washington Cathedral is one of the most beautiful churches in America.
華盛頓大教堂是美國最美麗的教堂之一。

⑤ **vicinity** [vəˋsɪnətɪ] (n.) 附近地區

例 The opera house is in the vicinity of the concert hall.
歌劇院就在音樂廳附近。

⑥ **parliament** [ˋpɑrləmənt] (*n.*) 議會；國會

例 If we're lucky, we'll have a chance to watch the parliament at work.

如果我們幸運的話，就有機會看到國會運作的方式。

⑦ **attend** [əˋtɛnd] (*v.*) 參加；出席

例 George wasn't able to attend any sporting events while he was in California.

喬治在加州時，不克參加體育活動。

⑧ **concert** [ˋkɑnsət] (*n.*) 音樂會；演奏會；演唱會

例 Tickets to the rock concert sold out in three hours.

這場搖滾演唱會的門票在三個小時內就賣光了。

⑨ **cultural** [ˋkʌltʃərəl] (*adj.*) 文化的；人文的

例 This guide book is full of cultural information about Thailand.

這本旅遊指南裡寫滿了泰國的文化資訊。

⑩ **entertainment** [͵ɛntəˋtenmənt] (*n.*) 娛樂；消遣

例 It's hard to imagine what kind of entertainment people have in that boring city.

很難想像那個無聊都市裡的人從事什麼樣的消遣娛樂。

受歡迎的觀光景點

| | | |
|---|---|---|
| **amusement park** | [əˋmjuzmənt ˋpɑrk] (n.) | 遊樂園 |
| **monument** | [ˋmɑnjəmənt] (n.) | 紀念碑；紀念建築物 |
| **national park** | [næʃənlˋpɑrk] (n.) | 國家公園 |
| **temple** | [ˋtɛmpl̩] (n.) | 寺廟 |
| **zoo** | [zu] (n.) | 動物園 |

受歡迎的文化活動

| | | |
|---|---|---|
| **opera** | [ˋɑpərə] (n.) | 歌劇 |
| **play** | [ple] (n.) | 戲劇 |
| **musical** | [ˋmjuzɪkl̩] (n.) | 歌舞劇 |
| **festival** | [ˋfɛstəvl̩] (n.) | 節慶；慶典 |
| **fair** | [fɛr] (n.) | 展覽會；廟會；市集 |

文化總匯

世界各大城市中，都會發行休閒娛樂雜誌。每週出版一次的週刊裡會報導所有的活動項目與時間，這些項目包含了電影、音樂、戲劇、演講、節慶、展覽、運動等等活動。以吟詩會為例，週刊裡會列出舉辦吟詩會的咖啡館，人們可以帶著自己創作的詩詞前往，在會中吟誦自己的創作。

# ✎ Exercises 動手做

請從以下字彙中，挑出正確的單字填入空格內。

| parliament | attraction | cathedral | |
|---|---|---|---|
| attend | vicinity | wonder | consider |

1. According to my guidebook, this _____ was built in 1476.

2. We should _____ our options carefully before making any decisions.

3. Do you ever _____ how the pyramids of Egypt were built?

4. I want to _____ at least one Chinese opera while I'm in Beijing.

5. Someone told me the Pompidou Center is in the _____ of Notre Dame Cathedral, but I can't find it.

1. 根據我的旅遊指南,這教堂建於一四七六年。
2. 做任何決定前,我們應該仔細考慮我們的選項。
3. 你曾納悶埃及金字塔是怎麼建起來的嗎?
4. 趁我還在北京時,我想最少要看一場京戲。
5. 有人告訴我龐畢度中心就在諾特丹教堂附近,但我就是找不到。

解答 1. cathedral 2. consider 3. wonder 4. attend 5. vicinity

## Preview 字彙預習

| | |
|---|---|
| **abstract** | 抽象的 |
| **aid** | 救助;幫助;援助 |
| **art gallery** | 藝廊;美術館 |
| **assist** | 協助;幫助 |
| **dlrect** | 給……指路;指出方向 |
| **directions** | 方向 |
| **exhibit** | 展示;展覽;陳列 |
| **exhibition hall** | 展覽廳 |
| **guide** | 引導;為……帶路 |
| **highlight** | 標示;強調 |
| **lost** | 迷路的 |
| **manage** | 處理;做到 |
| **map** | 地圖 |
| **museum** | 博物館;美術館 |
| **permanent** | 永久的;固定性的 |
| **point** | 指出 |
| **section** | 區域;區段 |
| **show room** | 陳列室 |
| **studio** | 畫室;雕塑室;工作室 |
| **trouble** | 麻煩;困擾 |

購票篇

*A tourist is buying tickets to the Louvre, in Paris.*

| | |
|---|---|
| Tourist: | Two tickets, please. |
| Ticket seller: | For two adults? |
| Tourist: | No, one adult and one child. Have you got a map of the museum? |
| Ticket seller: | Yes, here you are. It highlights the museum's main sections and the permanent exhibits. |
| Tourist: | Excellent. Thank you very much. |

翻譯

*一個觀光客正要買票進巴黎的羅浮宮美術館。*

觀光客：請給我兩張票。

售票員：兩張全票嗎？

觀光客：不，一張全票，一張孩童票。你這裡有美術館的**地圖**嗎？

售票員：有的，在這裡，它**標出**了美術館的主要**區域**和**常設展**。

觀光客：太棒了，非常謝謝你。

迷路篇

*A tourist loses his way in the Louvre.*

Tourist: Excuse me. I hate to trouble you, but I'm kind of lost.

Museum worker: Don't worry. It happens a lot here. Where do you need to go?

Tourist: I was looking for the abstract art area.

Museum worker: I'll give you directions. Exit this door, make a left, and walk to the stairwell. Go up the stairs to the second floor and you'll be there.

Tourist: I think I can manage that. Thanks for your help.

翻譯

*有個觀光客在美術館裡迷路了。*

觀光客　　　　　：對不起，我真的不想**麻煩**你。不過我好像**迷路**了。

美術館工作人員：別擔心，這裡常發生這種情況，你想去哪裡呢？

觀光客　　　　　：我在找**抽象**藝術區。

美術館工作人員：我來告訴你**方向**，出了這個門，左轉，走到樓梯間，往上到二樓，就到了。

觀光客　　　　　：我想我**辦得到**，謝謝你的幫忙。

1. **map** [mæp] (*n.*) 地圖

   例 We picked up a map of the city at the train station.
   我們在火車站拿了一份這個都市的地圖。

2. **highlight** [`haɪˌlaɪt] (*v.*) 標示；強調

   例 This guidebook highlights the main tourist attractions in the city.
   這本旅遊指南標出了這都市裡吸引觀光客的主要景點。

3. **section** [`sɛkʃən] (*n.*) 區域；區段

   例 What section of the museum do you want to see first?
   你想先看美術館裡的哪一區？

4. **permanent** [`pɜmənent] (*adj.*) 永久的；固定性的

   例 All of the paintings in this hall are on permanent display.
   這個廳裡的所有畫作都是固定的展覽品。

5. **exhibit** [ɪg`zɪbɪt] (*n.*) 展示；展覽；陳列

   例 The exhibit was so large we only had time to see half of it.
   這個展覽規模好大，我們的時間只夠看一半。

6 **trouble** [ˋtrʌb]] (*v.*) 麻煩；困擾

例 Could I trouble you to tell me the time?
可以麻煩你告訴我現在的時間嗎？

7 **lost** [lɔst] (*adj.*) 迷路的

例 If we follow the signs, we won't get lost.
如果我們跟著路標走，我們不會迷路的。

8 **abstract** [ˋæbstrækt] (*adj.*) 抽象的

例 Do you understand abstract art?
你懂抽象藝術嗎？

9 **directions** [dəˋrɛkʃəns] (*n.*) 方向

例 The store owner gave me directions to the bus station.
這個店家告訴我巴士站要怎麼走。

10 **manage** [ˋmænɪdʒ] (*v.*) 處理；做到

例 Can you manage carrying those bags by yourself?
你自己有辦法帶這些袋子嗎？

## 🖊 進階字彙

| | | |
|---|---|---|
| **museum** | [mju`zɪəm] (*n.*) | 博物館;美術館 |
| **art gallery** | [`ɑrt gælərɪ] (*n.*) | 藝廊;美術館 |
| **exhibition hall** | [ˌɛksə`bɪʃən `hɔl] (*n.*) | 展覽廳 |
| **show room** | [`ʃo `rum] (*n.*) | 陳列室 |
| **studio** | [`stjudɪˌo] (*n.*) | 畫室;雕塑室;工作室 |

| | | |
|---|---|---|
| **assist** | [ə`sɪst] (*v.*) | 協助;幫助 |
| **aid** | [ed] (*v.*) | 救助;幫助;援助 |
| **direct** | [də`rɛkt] (*v.*) | 給……指路;指出方向 |
| **guide** | [gaɪd] (*v.*) | 引導;為……帶路 |
| **point** | [pɔɪnt] (*v.*) | 指出 |

巴黎有很多很有名的美術館及博物館。其中的羅浮宮 (Louver) 是世界最知名的美術展覽館。羅浮宮原本是個皇宮,可看的東西本來就很多,再加上其收藏的藝術品,如果每件作品觀賞四十秒且晝夜不停地看,要花最少兩年的時間才有辦法看完。其收藏之豐富與多樣,讓很多旅行的人,只要一去巴黎就會去羅浮宮一飽眼福。

# ✏️ Exercises 動手做

請從以下字彙中，挑出正確的單字填入空格內。

| directions | permanent | highlights | |
|---|---|---|---|
| lost | manage | map | trouble |

1. When Sam got _____ in London, he asked a police officer for directions.

2. I'm not from this area, so I can't give you _____ to the post office.

3. We need to buy a _____ to help us get around the city.

4. If we hurry, we'll just _____ to make it to the train station on time.

5. I haven't got time to see everything, so I just need a brochure that _____ the best attractions.

1. 山姆在倫敦迷路時，他向警察問路。
2. 這個區域我不熟，所以我沒辦法告訴你郵局怎麼走。
3. 我們得買份地圖好在這個都市裡行動。
4. 如果我們快一點，我們就剛好可以準時到達火車站。
5. 我沒時間什麼都看，所以我需要一本標出最佳景點的手冊。

解答 1. lost  2. directions  3. map  4. manage  5. highlights

# Exercises 單字總復習 🔍 ✎

**A** 選一最適合的字完成下列句子

1. The bank threatened to take the man's home if he didn't pay his _____ on time.
   (A) vicinity
   (B) parliament
   (C) mortgage
   (D) exhibit

2. A good _____ can get you cheap airfares as well as cheap hotel rates.
   (A) travel agent
   (B) vending machine
   (C) rest stop
   (D) attraction

3. The children are trying to _____ their parents to take them to the amusement park.
   (A) convince
   (B) purchase
   (C) attend
   (D) wonder

4. The clear sky and mild temperature is _____ weather for a picnic.
   (A) permanent
   (B) abstract
   (C) weird
   (D) perfect

5. Since the _____ was delayed for several hours, the airline provided drinks and snacks to the waiting passengers.
   (A) beverage
   (B) cathedral
   (C) flight
   (D) relief

Millions of people enjoy traveling ____(1)____ , but not every traveler is alike. There are two main types. One enjoys the comfort and ease of joining a tour group. The major advantage of this method is the group takes care of everything, from transportation between the airport and the hotel, to arranging a(n) ____(2)____ , to setting up meals. Travelers can focus on enjoying themselves. The disadvantage to this method is group members have to follow the plan and don't have a chance to explore the country on their own.

The other type of traveler prefers independence. At the airport, they change money and find a way to the hotel. Then, using just a(n) ____(3)____ or guide book, they explore the place as they like. The major advantage to this method is freedom of movement. People ____(4)____ their own trips, going where they want and eating where they like. The main disadvantage is this can be very tiring. In fact, independent travelers sometimes compare their ____(5)____ to a full-time job!

1. (A) comfortable (B) abstract    (C) perfect    (D) abroad
2. (A) schedule    (B) entertainment (C) vicinity    (D) mortgage
3. (A) exhibit    (B) parliament    (C) directions (D) map
4. (A) wonder    (B) manage    (C) depart    (D) attend
5. (A) travel agent (B) journey    (C) section    (D) rest stop

解答

A 1. C  2. A  3. A  4. D  5. C

翻譯

1. 銀行揚言如果那個人不準時償還房貸，就要拿走他的房子。
2. 一個好的旅遊業者能幫你拿到便宜的機票和旅館房價。
3. 小孩子們正試著說服爸媽帶他們去遊樂園。
4. 晴朗的天空和宜人的溫度是最適合野餐的天氣。
5. 由於班機延遲了幾個鐘頭，航空公司提供飲料、點心給等候的旅客。

B 1. D  2. A  3. D  4. B  5. B

翻譯

許多人喜歡到國外旅遊，但是每個旅行者並不全然相似。主要的類型有兩種。一種喜歡參加旅行團的舒適、輕鬆。這種方式主要的優點是旅行團會打點好一切，從機場飯店間的接送、安排行程到安排餐點，旅客可以全心全意地享受。這種方式的缺點是團員必須按照計畫，沒有機會自己去探索那個國家。

另一種類型的旅行者偏好獨立自主。他們在機場兌換貨幣，自己想辦法到飯店去。之後，僅靠著一份地圖或是旅遊指南，他們就按自己喜歡的方式去探索那個地方。這種方式主要的優點是能自由行動。他們掌控自己的行程，去想去的地方、吃想吃的東西。主要的缺點是可能會很累人。事實上，自助旅行的人有時會把他們的旅程喻為一份全職的工作。

# 📖 Index 索引

294

國家圖書館出版品預行編目資料

多角建構英文字彙 / 白安竹作；-- 初版. -- 臺北市：
貝塔，2014. 08
面： 公分
ISBN: 978-957-729-968-0（平裝附光碟片）

1. 英語　2.詞彙

805.12　　　　　　　　　　　　　　　　　103014189

# 多角建構英文字彙

作　　者 / 白安竹
執行編輯 / 朱慧瑛

出　　版 / 貝塔出版有限公司
地　　址 / 台北市 100 中正區館前路 12 號 11 樓
電　　話 / (02)2314-2525
傳　　真 / (02)2312-3535
郵　　撥 / 19493777 貝塔出版有限公司
客服專線 / (02)2314-3535
客服信箱 / btservice@betamedia.com.tw

經　　銷 / 高見文化行銷股份有限公司
地　　址 / 新北市樹林區佳園路二段 70-1 號
客服專線 / 0800-055-365
傳真號碼 / 02-2668-6220

出版日期 / 2014 年 8 月初版一刷
定　　價 / 380 元
Ｉ Ｓ Ｂ Ｎ / 978-957-729-968-0

貝塔網址：www.betamedia.com.tw

喚醒你的英文語感！

Get a Feel for English !